Eternal Hues:

The Poetry Collection of Lotus Guan

(Bilingual Edition)

U0130654

Eternal Hues:

The Poetry Collection of Lotus Guan

(Bilingual Edition)

本色

關名君詩集

（中英典藏版）

Eternal Hues:

The Poetry Collection of Lotus Guan

(Bilingual Edition)

關名君

Lotus Guan

自序
Preface

我很喜歡《道德經》裡的一句話：「江海所以能為百谷王者，以其善下之 故能為百谷王。是以聖人欲上民，必以言下之；欲先民，必以身後之。是以聖人處上而民不重，處前而民不害，是以天下樂推而不厭。以其不爭，故天下莫能與之爭。」

小時候也經常用這段話鼓勵自己：
「故天將降大任於斯人也，必先苦其心志，勞其筋骨，餓其體膚，空乏其身，行拂亂其所為，所以動心忍性，曾益其所不能」在遇到困難或不開心的事情，我都會在心裡默默告訴自己：「一切都會好起來的，麵包會有的，牛奶也會有的，加油！所有的不開心都會煙消雲散，否極泰來！」

一直都想著把我的作品整理成詩詞集，在我有生之年再一首一首唱出來做成音樂專輯呈現給大家！真希望這個願望可以實現！
是的，我已經向前邁出了一小步了！
2018 年 5 月 2 日我的個人首張專輯《關關過》獻給大家了。

攜帶四首歌曲：《本色》

　　　　　　　《關關過》

　　　　　　　《親愛的你幸福嗎》

　　　　　　　《約定》

並於 2021 年 5 月 1 日發行個人首張 MTV《本色》希望大家可以喜歡、
2024 年發行《天下生蓮》單曲希望大家喜歡！

Preface

There is a line I like from Tao Te Ching,

"The sea gathers a hundred rivers because it lies low;
Because of its low position, it is the king over a hundred rivers.
He who desires to rise above the people must first humble himself;
He who desires to go before the people must first follow from behind.
Thus, when the Holy One rules above, people feel no burden;
When he leads, people are not harmed.
Therefore, the whole world gladly supports him and never tires of him.
He does not contend;
Therefore, no one in the world contends with him."

When I was young, I used to encourage myself with these words,

"When Heaven is about to confer a great office on any man, it first exercises his mind with suffering, and his sinews and bones with toil. It exposes his body to hunger, and subjects him to extreme poverty. It confounds his undertakings. By all these methods it stimulates his mind, hardens his nature, and supplies his incompetencies."

When I encounter difficulties or unhappy things, I will tell myself in my heart:
"Everything will be there. There will be bread, there will be milk. Come on! Let all the
trouble leave me forever. I'll be fine!"

I've always wanted to create a collection of my poems. Make them into a music album
and perform them as a song in my lifetime. I am looking forward to my wish coming
true!

It is happening now! I have taken a small step forward!
On the 2nd of May 2018, my first music album "Passing Through" was presented.

With four songs,
Eternal Hues: A Chronicle of Unchanging Essence
Passing Through
Are You Happy My Dear
Pledged Moments

On 1st May 2021, my first MTV "Eternal Hues: A Chronicle of Unchanging Essence"
released. Hope you will like it!

目錄
Contents

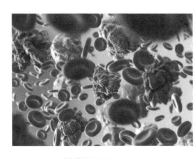

I

本色

Eternal Hues:
A Chronicle of
Unchanging Essence

2016 年 2 月 27 日

詞｜關名君　曲｜李東燊

飄然之間
靜觀自在
誰不想青春常在

奈何情深
奈何摯愛
誰曾在幕色徘徊

草木柔情
沙化蝶影
望丘壑數年積雪成澗

我非聖賢止望無間
天象環生
無大恨為寬

明鏡裡靜觀萬物變
唯本色之間

流水萬分身雨滴呈現
千山化數塵飄落不見

斗轉星移間
一年又一年
唯我本色永恆不變

歎那潮起花落不停歇
物是人非明月圓又缺

縱觀天地間
四季淪回變
唯我本色永恆不變

Everyone is yearning for the better to
dream on.

（每個人都在為了夢想實現不斷
努力）

Love and hate do not care too much.
（愛與恨都不必太牽掛）

Every minute of every day is an
experience and lost.
（每時每刻都在得到和失去）

When you understand the life true
meaning.
（當你領悟到生命的真諦）

Nothing will baffle you.
（任何事情都不能阻擋你）

草木柔情
沙化蝶影
望丘壑數年積雪成澗
我非聖賢止望無間

天象環生
無大恨為寬
明鏡裡靜觀萬物變
唯本色之間

流水萬分身雨滴呈現
千山化數塵飄落不見
斗轉星移間
一年又一年
唯我本色永恆不變

歎那潮起花落不停歇
物是人非明月圓又缺
縱觀天地間
四季淪回變
唯我本色永恆不變

緣來情去看世間滄桑
淚落間往事已成雲煙
情出善良念
鬢白朱顏改
唯我本色永恆不變　不變

I am no sage, my aspirations near,
Celestial patterns ever shifting, clear,
With no great resentment or heavy strife,
In the stillness of the mirror, I seek life.

Flowing waters, myriad forms they take,
Countless mountains, as dust, partake,
As constellations shift and time sweeps by,
Year after year, steadfast, I remain, I rely.

Amidst the drifting, serene and still,
Observing quietly, a tranquil thrill,
Who wouldn't yearn for eternal spring,
Where youthful bloom would forever sing?

Sighs escape as tides ebb and flowers wane,
Things change, yet the moon's phases remain,
Surveying the world, its vast expanse,
Seasons revolve, in perpetual dance.

But alas, emotions run deep,
Devoted love, a bond we keep,
Who among us hasn't wandered astray,
Lost in the twilight's enigmatic sway?

Amidst it all, unwavering, unswayed,
I remain true to my essence, unfrayed,
For within me, the colors of truth reside,
Eternal and unchanging, I confide.

The tender embrace of grass and tree,
Shadows of butterflies on sands set free,
Gazing at valleys where snow turns to stream,
Years of accumulation, a tranquil dream.

The ebb and flow of destiny's tide,

Memories fade, like mist they subside,

Kindness emanates, altering time's track,

Gray hair and altered beauty, a noble

fact.

In the realm of everlasting hues,

I hold steadfast, my essence I choose,

Through the cycles of this earthly realm,

Unyielding, unchanging, I stand at the

helm.

Fleeting connections, the world's grand

play,

Tears shed, memories fading away,

Love rooted in goodness, thoughts set

free,

While youth may fade, my essence shall

be.

2

幻藍
Azure Enchantment

2017 年 5 月 10 日

我問世界邊際在哪

我問大地會流淚嗎

我問藍天要個擁抱

我問明天還有多少

當雲飄向海望著山

當水流向田潤著麥

向簡單來句回應

用發現啟迪著失去

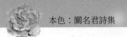
當黑雲飄入城市
黃沙滿天滿地
刺痛的臉龐
找著森林的方向

森林的淚潤著我
夾著我的淚一起留下
我比從前更加渴望
那幻藍色的天空

當沙粒再次被釋放
放下手中的一切
共同去抵擋
那狂風的掃蕩

Inquiring the world's farthest reaches,
Does the Earth shed its tears in breaches?
I ask the blue heavens for a warm
embrace,
I question how many tomorrows I'll
chase.

As clouds drift toward the vast sea's rim,
And waters flow, fields and crops to
trim,
In simplicity's whispers, I find my cue,
Discoveries enlighten the losses I rue.

When dark clouds loom over cityscape,
Yellow sands fill the sky, land, and drape,
Faces stung by the wind's icy knell,
Seeking the forest's path to dwell.

The forest's tears gently moisten me,
Entwined with my own, flowing free,
Yearning stronger than in days gone by,
For the illusion of a cerulean sky.

As grains of sand are set free once more,
I release all burdens I bore,
Together we stand, resilient and bold,
Defying the wild tempest's stranglehold.

3

如果千年
Echoes Across Millennia

2021 年 4 月 13 日 於香港

我從月亮上看下
藍色的星球多麼美
極光閃閃慢慢旋轉
星星點點的城市相連

如果千年不變
時間可以停下
我該如何對你說
——我愛你

我從雪山上看下
藍色的大海多麼美
白帆點點慢慢旋轉
海歐成群結隊飛舞

如果千年不變
時間可以停下
我該如何對你說
——我愛你

我拿著你的照片
燦爛的笑容多麼美
我的淚
止不住的流下
落在湖面凝成了冰

如果千年不變
時間可以停下
我該如何對你說
——我愛你

From the moon above, I gaze below,
The blue planet, a sight to behold.
Auroras shimmer, gracefully twirling,
Cities connected, stars softly unfurling.

If time could freeze, for a thousand years,
How could I express, my heart's deepest
fears?
How can I tell you, in words so true,
"I love you," forever, only for you.

From snowy peaks, I behold the seas,
Azure expanse, a captivating breeze.
Sails in the distance, spinning with grace,
Dolphins leaping, a mesmerizing chase.

If time could pause, for a thousand years,
How could I convey, emotions that
adhere?
How can I express, what's hidden within,
"I love you," eternally, our hearts akin.

I hold your photograph in my trembling
hand,
A radiant smile, beauty so grand.
My tears flow ceaselessly, unable to cease,
They fall upon the lake, frozen, in peace.

If time could stand still, for a thousand
years,
How could I utter, amid silent tears?
How can I whisper, what my heart longs
to say,
"I love you," forever, in every way.

4

遺憾
Remnants of Regret

2017 年 5 月 10 日

懷揣這一個不變的夢想
慢慢地走到懸崖之上
背著艱辛走到今天
我已滿心疲憊

幸福的定義太廣
無法形容的形狀
如果說十年時間是愛的刑場
我們都不用對彼此奢望

我願意在凌空的世界裡
與你的影子相伴
如果愛已經結出了果
我要為他創造個天堂

我可以犧牲一切去爭取
儘管我已滿身傷痕
如果你要轉身離去
沒人非要一起成長

我可以獨自一人
撐起一片天空

在你的背影畫上句號

With this unchanging dream held close,
I slowly tread upon the edge,
Bearing hardships to reach today,
My heart now weary and fatigued.

The definition of happiness, so vast,
Its shape beyond description's grasp.
If ten years' time is love's prison,
We need not hope extravagantly for each
other.

I am willing to dwell in a world ethereal,
Accompanied by the shadow of your
presence.
If love has already borne its fruit,
I shall create a heaven for it to reside.

I can sacrifice everything in pursuit,
Though my body bears scars deep and
wide.
If you choose to turn and depart,
No one insists on growing together side
by side.

I can stand alone,
Upholding a vast expanse of sky,
And mark the end with your fading
silhouette.

5

人生的意義
Echoes of Life's Essence

2023 年 6 月 2 日

兒時的記憶中最重要的
是媽媽臉上的笑容
給爸爸簽名的滿分試卷
妹妹搶走手裡的糖果
枝頭紅色蜻蜓顫動的翅膀
好想快點長大才最有意義

20 歲以後人生最重要的
寄給媽媽的生活費再多一些
體重再減一些可以報名比賽

又讀到了一首喜歡的詩詞
戴上結婚戒指的幸福時刻
第一次聽到新生命的心跳

40 歲之後生命最重要的
不被香煙和酒精迷幻而冷靜
在受到不公時還能保持善良
面對成功和失敗不驕不躁
面對父母保留兒時明亮的笑聲
乘風破浪勇往直前

60 歲之後生活最有意義的
每天可以按時睡著醒來
少一些疼痛多一些笑容
山間露珠烹煮的茶香
三五好友小聚暢談的時刻
體檢時多一些合格的指標
參加的婚禮比葬禮多

如果能有幸活到 100 歲
那是上天的眷顧
最重要的人生意義

每天看到太陽升起月亮升起
再次品嘗兒時懷念的味道
走在林間聞聞青草的馨香
再自由的呼吸新鮮的空氣
可以安詳的閉上雙眼
不再有痛苦了

In childhood's memory, most treasured
to me,
Mom's smiles, a heart's jubilee,
A perfect test, with Dad's proud embrace,
Sister's candy snatch, a sweet chase,
A crimson dragonfly's wings in flight,
Longing for adulthood's meaningful light.

Past twenty, life's importance anew,
More money sent, love shining through,
Shedding weight, for races to partake,
Discovering poems, passions awake,
Wedding ring worn, moments sublime,
First heartbeat heard, a life's chime.

After forty, life's essence takes hold,
Unswayed by smoke and spirits cold,
Kindness persists amidst unjust days,
Facing triumph and failure, calm always,
Parents' laughter, unchanged in time,
Venturing boldly, life's rhythm to climb.

Sixty and beyond, life's sweetness lies,
Restful sleep beneath starlit skies,
Less pain, more laughter, a morning
brew,
Friends gather, sharing tales anew,
Health indicators, a positive stride,
More weddings than funerals to ride.

If to reach a hundred years I'm graced,
Heaven's favor, a life embraced,
Daily sunrises, moons glowing bright,
Childhood flavors, rekindling delight,
Amidst the woods, scent of grass so fine,
Fresh air inhaled, freedom's sign,
A tranquil closure, eyes softly close,
Pain's release, a peaceful repose.

6

我的世界
Realms Within

2016 年 6 月 26 日

在沒有風　沒有雨　沒有陽光的
日子
我沒有哭　沒有笑　沒有流淚的
凝視
我的心情太平靜，聽得見呼吸的
振驚。
我是否還有明天，還有明天的明
天　也許……

流浪的腳步已經停下
流浪的心卻還在奔馳

我已記不清從哪天開始
又會在哪一天結束

哦我的世界是個無人認知的世界
廣袤無垠沒有邊際
時而冰雪滿天
時而風口浪尖

哦我的世界穿過人們冰冷的雙眼
曾幾何時你也會有同感
也想等待眼神交匯的瞬間
在包容名山大川和汪洋大海之後
是否容得下我的世界
我的世界

In days without wind, without rain,
without sunlight,
I neither cried nor laughed, with a gaze
unwept.
My emotions were too tranquil, hearing
the trembling of breath.

Do I still have a tomorrow, a tomorrow's
tomorrow, perhaps...

The wandering footsteps have ceased,
Yet the wandering heart still races.
I can no longer recall the day it began,
Nor the day it will end.

Oh, my world is an unknown world,
Vast and boundless, without limits.
Sometimes filled with ice and snow,
Sometimes amidst storms and gales.

Oh, my world passes through the cold
gaze of others,
At some point, you too may feel the
same.
Yearning for the moment when our eyes
meet,
After embracing towering mountains
and vast seas,
Will my world find a place,
In your accommodating embrace,
My world.

7

一千年的傷

A Millennium's Ache

2018 年 12 月 17 日

群山之中常見你的身影
吵吵間陪伴著我的歌聲
嬉戲中繞著你旋轉
寒風中漫步有你的陪伴

哦無論何時
你一直在這
靜靜聽我訴說
所有心聲
時光飛逝

慢慢改變一切
哦你還在這兒

驀然間發現你的堅強
風吹雨打也要挺起胸膛
默默堅持著不變的理想
真想長久成為你的模樣

屹立千年偉大的成長
如果十生十世後我們再相逢
決不會在樹幹上留下名字
給你代來一千年的傷

Amidst the mountains, your presence I
often see,
Whispers carry my songs alongside me.
Playfully, I spin around you,
In the cold wind, your companionship
remains true.

Oh, no matter when,

You have always been here,

Silently listening to my tales,

All the voices within my heart.

Time flies by,

Slowly changing everything,

Oh, but you are still here.

Suddenly, I discover your resilience,

Braving the winds and rains, standing tall.

Silently persisting in your unchanging ideals,

I yearn to become just like you, lasting and true.

Standing tall, a thousand years of great growth,

If we meet again after ten lives, ten reincarnations,

We will never carve our names upon the tree trunk,

I will bear a thousand years of hurt for you.

8

最後一片葉子

The Last Leaf's Embrace

2018 年 12 月 27 日

最後一片葉子

好像所有他的驕傲與自豪

透過陽光的色彩

亮出金黃的成功色

潤著溫柔的月光

沉浸在幸福之中

最後一片葉子

孤零零地在樹上

他的驕傲已經消失了

看著地上的夥伴在瑟瑟發抖
他的幸福也消失了
漸漸的地上的夥伴也都消失了

最後一片葉子
在寒風凜冽中跳著舞蹈
迎接春天的到來
慢慢的他腳下癢一癢
小小的樹芽鑽了出來
在一個春雨滋潤的夜晚

最後一片葉子
抱著小小的樹芽
笑著他有了新的夥伴
風搖曳著他瘦瘦的身子
吹散了他最後一絲經脈
他抱著小小的樹芽
給她最後一個長長的吻

隨著細細的風
慢慢的轉著圈圈

悠悠蕩蕩地落在地上
慢慢的含著笑閉上了眼睛

我來到他的身旁
拾起這最後一片葉子
擦乾他身上的雨水
慢慢的放在我的書裡面
讓他曾經的驕傲陪伴著我
讓他曾經的幸福和笑陪伴著我
從此你不再孤單！

In the realm of the falling leaf,
Where pride and honor find relief,
Through hues of sunlight, a vivid display,
Glimmers of golden triumph hold sway,
Bathed in gentle moonlight's embrace,
Enveloped in a blissful, tranquil space.

The final leaf upon the tree,
Stands alone, a poignant decree,
Its pride has faded, lost and gone,

While fellow companions tremble upon,
Its happiness, too, has drifted away,
Slowly vanishing, as if to say,

In the icy winds, it dances and sways,
Welcoming the arrival of brighter days,
A tiny itch tickles beneath its feet,
A tender sprout emerges, so petite,
On a night drenched in spring's sweet
rain,
A tiny bud, a fragile domain.

The final leaf cradles the budding friend,
Smiling, a new bond they gently blend,
The wind sways its slender, frail frame,
Dispersing the last remnants, its claim to
fame,
It embraces the sapling with a loving
grace,
Bestowing a final, lingering embrace.

With a gentle breeze's delicate twirl,
In circling motion, it begins to unfurl,

Descending leisurely, landing on the
ground,
Closing its eyes with a contented sound,

I draw near to its lonely side,
Lifting the final leaf with utmost pride,
Wiping away the raindrops that cling,
Placing it carefully in my cherished thing,
May its past pride accompany me,
Its happiness and laughter forever be,
No longer shall you be alone, forlorn and
astray.

9

嵐海
Mists of the Sea

2019 年 3 月 13 日

清新的風扶面而來
波光粼粼白鷺飛翔
絲絲花香泌著心肺
溫暖陽光灑向四方

一縷七色光中含苞放
鳥兒自由的飛翔
希望的眼神透露閃光
美好的時光這裡生長

儘管諸多不如意
永遠不要放棄希望
生命本身就是奇跡
不要再想傷害自己
時間會撫平所有的傷
伸出雙手擁抱每天的朝陽

A fresh breeze gently caresses the face,
Shimmering waves, white herons take
flight,
Silken flower scents, the heart does
embrace,
Warm sunlight spills its grace, day and
night.

Within a ray of seven colors, buds unfold,
Birds soar freely, their spirits take flight,
Eyes full of hope, a sparkling story told,
Moments of beauty bloom here, so
bright.

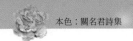
Though life may be filled with struggles
and woes,
Never abandon the hope that ignites,
For life itself is a wondrous prose,
Banish self-harm, embrace the guiding
lights.

Time, a gentle mender, will heal every
hurt,
Reach out your hands, let the sunrise
invite,
Embrace each day, let love be your assert,
In its golden rays, find strength and
delight.

IO

為愛而生
Born for Love

2019 年 3 月 28 日

漸漸的明白風的意義
輕扶著白色的雲
享受著春的腳步
漸漸的喜歡細雨濛濛
霧化著每一座城
我要好好努力為愛而生

我尋尋覓覓享受
我跌跌撞撞奔去
我迷迷茫茫自問
我瀟瀟灑灑追尋

我小小心心傾聽
我這一生為愛而生！

漸漸發現已走過半生
還要轟轟烈烈度過這一世
日日夜夜都在重生
漸漸明白自己真正在乎的
是傾聽內心深處的真與善
我要轟轟烈烈為愛而生
是的
我的這一生為愛而生！

Slowly grasping the essence of the wind,
Gently caressing the clouds so white,
Embracing the steps of spring, a joy to
find,
Gradually, I fall for drizzles' misty light.

A veil of fog shrouds each cityscape,
Seeking, I strive, for love to ignite,

Amidst uncertainties, my heart finds its
shape,
Chasing dreams, I venture with all my
might.

Listening closely, with a heart that's pure,
This life devoted to love's delight,
Half a lifetime passed, yet courage
endures,
Embracing each day, with passion
burning bright.

Through days and nights, a cycle reborn,
Discovering what truly matters inside,
The essence of goodness, from within is
drawn,
With fervor and fire, for love, I will
abide.

Yes, indeed,
This life of mine is born for love's grand
stride!

II

表像
Facade of Reality

2020 年 12 月 18 日

重複著相同的節奏
呼吸著　凝視著
來來回回　我不停穿梭
目光中還帶著虔誠
如果沒有敷衍的應和
內心是否多一分開朗
如果重新來過中清醒
我的等待每一秒都值得

清晰地聽見心跳的節奏
感受千里之外的等待

反反覆覆意念的空間
我不會被表像所迷惑
如果時間停止在今天
不會後悔那一瞬的相遇
如果你也從來沒有改變
真心的期盼永恆的陪伴

是的　表像不被矇騙

啊　我們還有明天

Repeating the same rhythm, a dance in
my soul,
Breathing and gazing, my heart feels
whole,
Back and forth, I endlessly roam,
With reverence in my gaze, I search for
my goal.

If not met with mere complacent reply,
Would my inner self beam with a
brighter light?

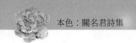

If given the chance to start anew, no lie,
Every second of my waiting, worthwhile,
so right.

Clearly hearing the heartbeat's melody,
Feeling the distance, the wait so wide,
In the space of thoughts, looping
continuously,
I won't be deceived by mere appearances'
pride.

If time could freeze at this very day,
No regrets for that fleeting encounter's
sway,
If you remained unchanged, come what
may,
Sincerely hoping for eternal togetherness,
I pray.

Indeed, appearances won't cloud my
sight,
Ah, there's still tomorrow, a shining ray.

12

此刻就是幸福
Now is Happiness

2021 年 4 月 13 日

慢步海邊輕風陣陣
淺淺的藍淡淡的鹽
微微的霧輕輕的雲
此時此刻就是幸福

繁華的城市有你
擁擠的街道有我
徘徊的路口有他
此時此刻就是幸福

我的笑眼中有你
你的淚水中有我

他的思念中有她
此時此刻就是幸福

我在月亮上看著你
你在星星上看著我
他在太陽的影子中
此時此刻就是幸福

如果我還有很多明天
如果你不在懊悔昨天
如果他笑著面對明天
此時此刻就是幸福

In the bustling city, I find you there,
Crowded streets, in my steps, I share,
At the crossroads, he lingers with care,
In this very moment, happiness is rare.

My laughing eyes hold you tight,
Your tears, within them, find their light,
His longing heart, her sight,
In this very moment, happiness feels
right.

I gaze at you from the moon so high,
You watch me from stars in the sky,
He resides in the sun's shadowed sigh,
In this very moment, happiness amplifies.

Strolling slowly by the seaside, gentle
winds embrace,
Shallow blue waters, a hint of salt's
embrace,
Subtle mists, tender clouds' trace,
In this very moment, happiness we
embrace.

If many tomorrows still await my sight,
If no regrets dwell in your past's twilight,
If he smiles bravely at tomorrow's height,
In this very moment, happiness feels so
right.

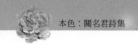

I3

不想説話
Silent Serenity

2020 年 6 月 18 日

不想說話
對視的眼神
只想牽著你的手
一起走在風雨後
彩虹出現在天邊

不想說話
默默看著你的笑臉
彼此依偎著抱緊
請你閉上雙眼
嘴角上含著笑甜蜜

不想說話
望著遠處的朝陽
應著我們紅紅的臉
也許我們的永遠
讓時間停在彼此之間

不想說話
就這樣緊緊抱著你
深深的呼吸甜甜的空氣
閉上雙眼去感受
此刻幸福的味道

In silence, our eyes meet, no words to be
spoken,
I only want to hold your hand, unbroken,
Walking together through the rain's
token,
A rainbow appears as love's true omen.

No words needed, just your smiling face,
In each other's arms, we find solace's
embrace,

Please close your eyes, feel love's embrace,
Sweet laughter lingers on lips, love's
grace.

No words to be said, the sun on the
horizon,
Our faces blushing, love's colors horizon,
Perhaps, our forever, an eternal liaison,
Time halts between us, an immortal
garrison.

No words needed, tightly holding you
near,
Inhaling sweet air, love's atmosphere,
With closed eyes, this bliss we revere,
The taste of happiness, this moment's
premiere.

14

重生
Rebirth

什麼是真的
什麼是假的

什麼是對的
什麼又是錯的

什麼是好的
什麼是壞的

什麼是你的
什麼又是我的

明明真的是心痛
卻流不下一滴淚

本想輕輕鬆鬆放下
卻隱隱墜入谷底心河

閉上眼睛
誰又出現在我的腦海
心裡的恨
漸漸忘卻了是是非非
如果可以重生
我還會做出同樣的選擇嗎
是的
我無悔
如果可以重生
我會重新學會愛你
是的
毫無保留
傾盡所有

What is real, and what is mere facade?
What is right, and what's deemed flawed?
What is good, and what's in claws of bad?
What belongs to you, and what's mine,
untrod?

Clearly, it's heartache that I endure,
Yet, not a single tear can I procure,
I thought I could let go, secure,
But I find myself falling into love's
obscure.

Closing my eyes, a figure appears,
In my mind, resentment's ancient spears,
Fading away, the truth becomes unclear,
As shades of right and wrong disappear.

If rebirth were a gift, a chance anew,
Would I repeat the same course, stay
true?
Yes, without regrets, my heart's eschewed,
In this life and beyond, my love for you.

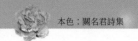
If reborn, I'd learn to love with might,
With open heart, unguarded and bright,
In this journey of love's flight,
With all my being, I'd hold you tight.

This enigma of life, its twists and turns,
Through joys and sorrows, the heart
discerns,
With love's strength, the fire burns,
In this world of uncertainties, love
adjourns.

15

追趕
Chasing Horizons

2018 年 4 月 5 日

我追趕著太陽
她對我說
我們太過遙遠

我追趕著月亮
她對我說
我太過寒冷

我追趕著明天
她對我說
請你珍惜今天

我追趕著時間
她對我說我們隔著永恆

我不停地追趕
結果還站在原點

我不服命運的安排
不會停下前進的腳步

逆著狂風推著我
劃破我的臉龐

翻過一座座高山
來到世界之巔
伸出雙手接受晨光的洗禮
代表著至高無上的榮耀

I chase after the sun's golden rays,
She whispers to me, we're too far away,
I pursue the moon's ethereal embrace,
She murmurs, I'm too cold, my heart
astray.

I chase after the morrow's unknown,
She pleads, cherish today's love we own,
I chase after time, an eternity to atone,
She reminds, we're separated, distance
sown.

Relentlessly, I chase without reprieve,
Yet find myself at the starting sleeve,
Defying fate's design, I won't deceive,
Never halting my steps, I believe.

Against fierce gales, they push me ahead,
Scarring my face, a journey widespread,
Over towering mountains, where paths
tread,
Reaching the world's summit, I'm not
misled.

I reach out my hands to embrace dawn's
light,
In its glory, I stand, an endless height,
A symbol of honor, bathed in morning's
might,
With supreme splendor, my spirit takes
flight.

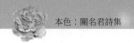

16

克米族的小金鋼

The Little Iron Guardian of Kemi Clan

2023 年 4 月

在平行時間的交界處
有一個克米世界小人族
各種顏色小矮人的故鄉
一個紫色的小金鋼跳到樹冠
瞭望著遠處的飛船動向

他臉上塗著黑色的偽裝
深深的雙眼明亮遠望
手中握著號角隨時通知同伴

他的職責是那麼重要
肚子餓了兩天在打鼓
他幾乎忘記絲毫不受影響

他的名字是族長取的
小金鋼是全族的驕傲
他把身體趴在一片樹葉上
巨大的螞蟻從他身邊爬過

他拿起長槍刺向螞蟻胸部
一陣風吹過他跳向另一片樹葉
他趴在樹葉上一動也不動
就像一座豐碑屹立不倒

他是全族的希望和榮耀
他會堅持到底絕不放棄
誓死守護他的美好家園

At the junction of parallel time's
embrace,
A realm of small beings, the Kemi race,
In hues of colors, their home finds grace,
A purple steel gnome ascends to trace.

His face adorned with a mask of night,
Bright eyes shimmer, gazing far and wide,
A horn in hand, a signal to incite,
His duty paramount, none can deride.

For two days hungry, yet undeterred,
He beats the drums, his resolve conferred,
Oblivious to hunger's tempest stirred,
In adversity's storm, he stands unblurred.

Chieftain named him, Little Steel his
might,
A pride, the tribe holds dear and bright,
On a leaf, he rests, a steadfast sight,
A giant ant crawls by, a fleeting flight.

With spear in hand, he strikes with
might,
As winds gust, he leaps, a nimble flight,
Upon the leaf, motionless in light,
An unyielding monument, he ignites.

The hope and glory of his kin's array,
Never faltering, come what may,
He swears to protect, without delay,
His cherished homeland, forever to stay.

17

還好沒有一錯到底

Guided by Hope, Errors Undone

還好沒有一錯到底
是什麼綁住了我的腳步
是什麼迷惑了我的心志
是什麼讓我失去了方向
是什麼醉得我無法醒來

還好沒有一錯到底
明天又是一個嶄新的自我

重生般明亮的心
打開了一扇窗
一縷陽光洗去了
我一身的傷痕

感謝未來期許中的自己
沒有什麼比希望
更能喚醒沉睡中的我
就算精疲力盡也無所謂

還好沒有一錯到底
至少我還有希望的燈
照亮我那嶄新的人生

還好沒有一錯到底
睜開眼看見的是黎明
推開門擁抱太陽的親吻

Fortunate, no mistakes to mar,
Yet something binds my steps afar,
Confusion clouds my resolute star,

Lost, I wander, direction ajar,
Intoxicated, I can't break the scar.

Fortunate, no mistakes to scar,
Tomorrow's a self, renewed and bizarre.

Rebirthed, a brightened heart's debut,
A window opens, revealing the view,
Sunlight's embrace, my wounds undo,
Grateful for the future's rendezvous.

Hope beckons from the days ahead,
Awakening me from slumber's bed,
Even in exhaustion, nothing to dread,
For hope's power, my spirit is fed.

Fortunate, no mistakes to obscure,
A beacon of hope, my path secure,
Illuminating life, a fresh allure.

Fortunate, no mistakes to deride,
At dawn's awakening, my eyes wide,
Embracing the sun's tender stride.

18

就讓時間停止在此刻

Moments Frozen in Eternity

當時間停止在此刻
如果是心痛得無法呼吸
如果愛你的心還沒停下
如果不知不覺就落下眼淚
真想時間停止在此刻的我們

重複著當初的相遇時刻
望著初見你時驚詫的眼神
握著你冰冷的雙手發呆
你為我披著第一件外套

閉著雙眼初吻你的唇
夢中重複出現你的笑臉
我真的該拿你怎麼辦啊
就讓時間停止在此刻
化作流星變成永恆吧

如果淚滴化作一顆珍珠
如果回到最初相遇的時刻
如果我會不知不覺的愛上你
就讓時間停止在此刻的我們

我們的愛化作太陽的光芒
此時此刻化作永恆不變
慶倖還能再次遇見如此的你
握緊你的雙手從此不在放開

When time, at this moment, could cease,
If heartache hinders breath's release,
If love's beat persists, in steady peace,
Tears fall unseen, yearning for release,
I wish time would freeze, our love
increase.

Revisiting the moment we first met,
Gazing, astonished, eyes so beset,
Holding your hands, ice-cold, no regret,
You draped your coat, a love duet.

With eyes closed, our lips entwine,
In dreams, your smiling face aligns,
What to do with you, feelings so divine,
Let time stand still, a celestial sign,
A shooting star, forever, we'll enshrine.

If tears could crystallize, pearl-bright,
If we could rewind to that starlit night,
Unknowingly, I fell, love's pure delight,
Let time pause, in this serenade of light.

Our love turns to the sun's radiant ray,
In this moment, eternal, it'll stay,
Grateful to meet you once more today,
In your hands, forever, I'll convey.

19

股市風雲

Stock Market Symphony

2023 年 6 月 28 日 多雲

一個無聲的戰場
在虛幻的世界
無數的精英
參與其中

沒有刀光劍影
卻有血肉橫飛
沒有槍林彈雨
卻有滿心傷痕

有如大浪淘沙
一年又一年的進
一年又一年的退
是勝是敗都是英雄
是對是錯歷史見證

百年的沉浮中
周線月線年線
譜寫萬里江山圖
雷電交加聲聲不斷

時而風雨飄搖
時而晴空萬里
時而滿堂喝彩
時而全線潰敗

誰才是常勝將軍
你我拭目以待

A soundless battlefield, it lies,
In a realm of dreams, where shadows rise,
Countless elites, their skills comprise,
In this ethereal realm, they harmonize.

No clashing swords, nor gleaming spears,
Yet, blood and flesh, the heartache bears,
No gunfire roars, yet scars appear,
A canvas of wounds, emotions steers.

Like sands sifted in a grand design,
Year after year, advances entwine,
Victory or defeat, both define,
History witnesses the battle's sign.

Through centuries' ebb and flow,
Weekly, monthly, yearly show,
Writing the saga of lands below,
Thunder and lightning, echoes grow.

Sometimes storms and tempests churn,
Other times, clear skies return,
Applause resounds, hearts yearn,
Or all lines crumble, lessons learned.

Who, then, holds victory's crown?
With bated breath, we look around.

20

放過你也放過我自己

Release You, Release Myself

是什麼時候
我們變成這樣
熱淚流不停
心裡結了冰

一句結束的話
震驚的表情
沒有你的明天
還算是明天嗎

如果這就是結局
我有多麼不開心
如果這些都是假像
為什麼有真實的開始

放過你也放過我自己
給你想要的自由
也給自己一個自由
全新的世界

心裡不管有多麼不捨
至少我們會成為朋友

放過你也放過我自己
就當是一個美好的夢
從此刻破碎

我們都有追求美好的權利
廣闊的天空任你我遨遊

When did we change, oh, pray tell,

Tears flow ceaseless, hearts in icy shell,

One ending phrase, faces shocked and
swell,

Without you, is tomorrow truly a
farewell?

In pursuit of beauty, we hold the right,

Vast skies await, for both to take flight.

If this is the conclusion we unfold,

How unhappy I feel, the story foretold,

If all is but illusion, a tale retold,

Why did a genuine beginning take hold?

Setting you free, I'll free myself too,

Granting you the freedom you're due,

And gifting myself a freedom anew,

A world reborn, a vision to pursue.

Though reluctance fills my heart's hollow,

At least, we'll remain friends, no sorrow.

Setting you free, I'll free myself too,

Treasure this dream, where our hearts
once grew,

From this moment, let it shatter and
subdue.

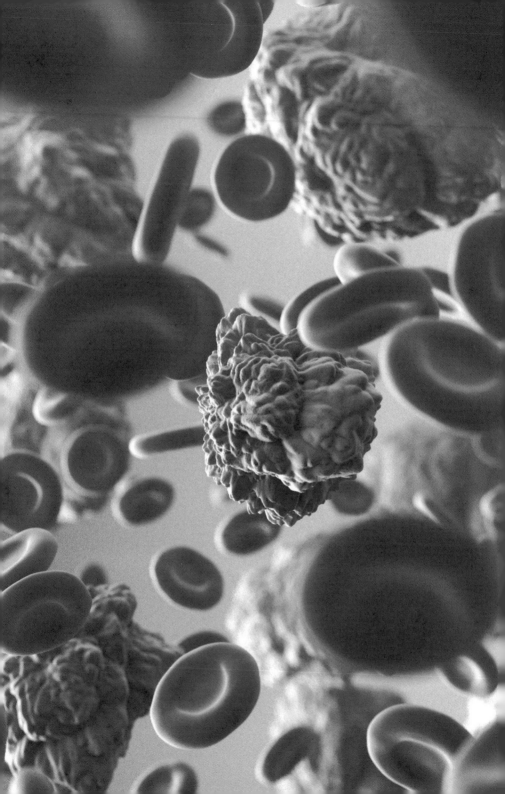

21

微觀世界
Microcosm's Reverie

2021 年 4 月 26 日

在無限放大中
來到微觀世界

我成了我身體的國王
億萬精靈的主宰

心跳的核心動力
舞動著紅色軍團

每一口呼吸著興奮
每一個心靈電光交匯

每一個細胞的忠誠
每一個無比的信任

我不會再為無謂的事
傷害這些弱小的士兵

我不會消耗心神痛苦傷心
我的心靈仿佛瞬間昇華

從前的糾結豁然開朗
曾經重要的一切都不再重要

帶領我的萬千子民
重獲新生

善待每一個細胞對我的忠誠
感謝你們的無私奉獻
周而復始　任勞任怨

在我的王國每天歡慶節日
感慨生命的真諦
創造無限奇跡可能

In the realm of boundless magnification,
Into the microcosm, a wondrous
expedition,

I became the sovereign of my own
domain,
Ruler of myriad spirits, a celestial reign.

The heartbeat's core, a pulsating force,
Dancing scarlet legions, a poetic
discourse,

Each breath a thrill, excitement untold,
Minds' electric symphony, a spectacle of
gold.

In each cell's allegiance, loyalty so true,
Unwavering trust, an eternal debut,

No more shall I harm these fragile
knights,
Their valor embraced, igniting new
heights.

No longer drained by sorrow's remorse,

My spirit ascends, an ethereal course,

Past entanglements, now gleaming and
clear,
What once mattered most, now fading,
my dear.

Guiding my people, a multitude so
grand,
Rebirth enkindled, across the land,

Cherishing cells, their devotion
profound,
Gratitude for selfless gifts, hearts
unbound.

Through cycles relentless, with diligence
and grace,
In my kingdom's embrace, celebrations
trace,

Reflecting on life's essence, a wistful
embrace,
Unveiling boundless wonders,
possibility's grace.

22

日出
Dawn's Embrace

一團火紅跳出海面
溫暖著寒冷的大地
喚醒了沉睡的萬物

激蕩起千層波瀾
疊吸著萬層雲朵

群山聳立倒影巍屹
群芳轉頭向你綻放

照亮著每一處黑暗
溫暖著受傷的心靈

無限光芒萬丈

田裡的麥向你低頭
樹上的葉向你招手

枝頭的花向您撫媚
叢間的蝶向你舞蹈

孩子笑臉上印著火紅的光
你是我心中的崇拜和嚮往
太陽之神——
億萬年不變的永恆之光

A burst of fiery red emerges from the sea,
Warming the frigid earth, setting it free,
Awakening dormant life from slumber
deep,
In its radiant glow, secrets it shall keep.

Ripples cascade, a thousand layers high,
Absorbing clouds that paint the sky,

Mountains stand tall, mirrored below,
Blossoms turn, their vibrant colors show.

Darkness is banished by its golden
embrace,
Healing wounded souls, a tender grace,
Infinite brilliance, a beacon so grand,
A sunlit realm, forever to withstand.

Wheat bows down in fields aglow,
Leaves wave gently, a friendly hello,
Flowers on branches, their allure unfold,
Butterflies dance, a story untold.

Children's laughter imprinted in red and
gold,
You are my admiration, a tale of old,
O Sun God, unwavering and bright,
Eternal light, through day and night.

23

忘記我是誰
Forgotten Identity

2016 年 8 月 29 日

看著你的笑臉　我笑了
看著你在流淚　我哭了
清晨睜開眼是你的睡眼矇矓
我的心一下子安定了下來

每天二十四小時的陪伴
心中只關心你的寒與暖
風和雨繫著我對你的牽掛
一步一步看著你繼續向前

哦　想你想你想你想你
見不到你我坐立不安
急迫的心激動不已

哦　念你念你念你念你
安心把你擁有入懷裡
再多的艱辛與孤寂
也不能把你我分離

哦　喚你喚你喚你喚你
朗朗的笑聲　沁入我心底
我的昨天和明天徹底變成了你

過去和未來　我已不復存在
只留下那句最美的遺言
重複說著千遍
媽媽愛你到永遠！永遠

Gazing upon your smiling face, I'm
aglow,
Tears in your eyes, my own overflow,

In the morning's haze, as you rise from
sleep,
Calm settles within, emotions run deep.

Twenty-four hours, side by side,
Your warmth and comfort, my heart's
guide,
Wind and rain, they bear my care,
Watching you forge ahead, step by daring
step, rare.

Oh, how I long for you, day and night,
Restless when you're out of sight,
Anxious heart, a fervent plea,
Yearning for you, an urgent decree.

Oh, I think of you, a constant refrain,
In my embrace, you'll always remain,
No matter the hardships, the lonely ride,
You and I, forever intertwined.

Oh, I call to you, a joyous sound,
Laughter's echo, within me bound,
My yesterdays and tomorrows, they
cease,

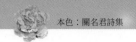

In you, my present, my heart finds its

peace.

Past and future, I no longer roam,
Leaving behind a legacy, a cherished

poem,
Repeating, a thousand times and more,
Mom, I love you forever, to the core.

24

幸福擔當
Bearer of Bliss

2017 年 5 月

塗個指甲再燙個頭髮

抖抖肩膀嚼個口香糖

口紅塗上什麼顏色才好呢？

每天都有個新造型

只要你眼前一亮

這也是我心所向

一天實現一個小小願望

紅酒醉人的迷香

絲絲甜味心蕩漾

你溫柔的目光給我無盡能量
就希望時間凝固此時的幸福

你的表白深深印在我心房
不奢望所有夢想都能如願啊
只要有你在身旁
這一個就足夠
你和我一樣

讓我們手牽手一起看朝陽
未來的每一天讓幸福來擔當
風和雨讓彩虹映襯出美好
再來一起看夕陽

Painting nails and styling hair,
Shoulder shakes and gum to spare,
Lipstick's hue, which shade to find?
A new look daily, hearts intertwined.

With every glance, your eyes alight,
My heart finds solace, in purest light,

In each new style, a wish unfurled,
In your gaze, a transformed world.

A fragrance of wine, intoxicates the air,
A subtle sweetness, beyond compare,
Your gentle eyes, a wellspring deep,
Moments frozen, in memories we keep.

Your confession, etched upon my soul,
Dreams may falter, yet hearts are whole,
By your side, my beacon, my guide,
In your presence, all doubts subside.

Hand in hand, we face the dawn,
Embracing futures yet to be drawn,
Rain and wind, a rainbow's dance,
Together, we watch the sun's last glance.

25

喜歡你

Whispers of Affection

2021 年 3 月 27 日

甜甜的蛋糕
甜甜的蜜

甜甜的奶茶
甜甜的笑

玫瑰的艷紅簇一團火
倒映著紅燭的光搖曳
映襯著鑽石的閃耀

我想大聲說——我喜歡你
大聲說出許久以來的心意

我想大聲說我喜歡你
浪漫的話語羞澀的你

喜歡你的笑每分每秒
喜歡你的每一個胡鬧

七彩煙火映著你的微笑
熾熱的眼神中只有你

深深的吻著你的唇
沒有什麼可以阻擋我愛你

今後餘生我們真愛相伴
攜手共赴美好的明天

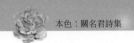

Sweet, sweet cake,
Sweet, sweet honey,
Sweet, sweet milk tea,
Sweet, sweet laughter.

Roses ablaze in crimson fire,
Candlelight's glow, a flickering pyre,
Diamonds shine, reflecting light,
In this moment, our love takes flight.

I long to proclaim - "I cherish you,"
Words unspoken, now coming true,
Loud and clear, my heart's desire,
A confession, set free from its wire.

I want to say aloud, "I'm fond of you,"
Romantic words, whispered by you,
I adore your laughter, each moment, each
second,
Every playful act, I am recklessly
beckoned.

Fireworks of colors, in your smile they
play,
In your passionate gaze, I'll always stay,
Kissing your lips, deep and sincere,
Nothing can hinder, our love's frontier.

In the days ahead, our love shall thrive,
Hand in hand, through life we'll strive,
For a beautiful tomorrow, side by side,
Our genuine love, an endless ride.

26

平凡的我
Ordinary Brilliance

2021 年 4 月 27 日

也許我沒有俊美的外表
也許我沒有顯赫的家世
也許我沒有高大的體格
也許我沒有出眾的才華

但請相信我平凡絕不平庸

就算像沙粒一樣渺小
我也要擁抱大海
就算像塵埃一樣無重
我也要屹立於山頂之上

沒有誰能生來就偉大

我相信我去相信的
我追逐我去追逐的
我成就我所有的夢想
我造就無畏而平凡的我

時間是運動著的鐘擺
我願每天的十萬次心跳
宣誓生命的豪言壯語
無論過去還是未來
我—就是我
平凡的生命開出燦爛的花朵

Perhaps no handsome visage is mine to
show,
Perhaps no grand lineage for the world
to know,
Maybe not towering stature, strong and
wide,
Maybe no dazzling talent by my side.

But trust, I am no ordinary, I'm resolute,
In me, there's more than meets the eye's
pursuit,
Like a grain of sand, though small and
fine,
I'll embrace the ocean, let my spirit shine.

Though dust may scatter, weightless in
the breeze,
I'll stand atop mountains, heart unceased,
No one is born with greatness innate,
Yet belief can conquer, it's never too late.

I trust in what I choose to trust,
I chase what's worthy, never unjust,
I'll achieve dreams that are truly mine,
Forge fearlessness and rise, unconfined.

Time's pendulum swings, ceaseless and
bright,
My heartbeat, a cadence of unyielding
might,
I pledge to life's promise, loud and clear,
Past and future unite, I'm boldly here.

I am who I am, in this moment, this
space,
A life unremarkable, yet a vibrant grace,
Just like a flower, ordinary and true,
Blooming brilliantly, a life anew.

27

我的天堂
My Paradise

2021 年 4 月

如果有那麼一個地方
在遙遠的阿爾法星球上
時空之門帶我來到這裡
這就是我的天堂

粉紅色的天空
粉紅色的城
芬芳的空氣
淡紫色的山
魚兒飛在我頭上

沒有痛苦和寒冷
沒有仇恨和罪惡
只有無盡的真誠和善良
只有永遠的忠誠和美好
我來到了我的天堂

淡藍色的星空
粉紅色的雲
溫暖的輕風
扶著淡紫色的海
鳥兒落在我手上

沒有差異和不公
沒有艱辛和淚水
只有無盡平等和祥和
只有永遠幸福和美好
我來到了我的天堂

In a place, perhaps, exists afar,

On Alpha's planet, a radiant star,

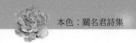

Through the gateway of space and time,
This haven's realm, uniquely mine.

A pink-hued sky, a city so fair,
Fragrant breezes kiss the air,
Lavender peaks, a gentle sight,
Fish aloft, in ethereal flight.

No pain or cold, in this abode,
No hatred's grip, no sin bestowed,
Endless kindness, sincere and true,
Everlasting beauty, loyalty too,
In my own paradise, I now reside.

Azure stars in a canvas vast,
Pink clouds whisper as they drift past,
Warm winds guide with tender touch,
Over a lilac sea, they gently clutch,
Birds alight in the palm of my hand.

No divides, no injustice here,
No toil, no tears, no looming fear,
Unending peace, a tranquil grace,
Eternal joy, in this embrace,
In my paradise, I firmly stand.

28

愛
Eternal Love

2021 年 2 月

愛是無私的付出
愛是漫長的等待
愛是街邊的棉花糖
愛是送你蝴蝶髮夾

愛是為你毫無保留
愛是為你傾盡所有
愛是為你赴湯蹈火
愛是你的眼裡只有我

愛是深夜為你留的那盞燈
愛是媽媽手中的紅蘋果

愛是女兒那清脆的笑聲
愛是枝頭追逐的雙蝶

愛是我們緊握的雙手
愛是我們無盡的流浪
愛是帶著你踏遍群山

此時此刻
愛是我能遇到你
翻著動人的詩篇

Love's a lantern, burning bright,
In the depths of night, its guiding light,
An apple from a mother's hand,
A daughter's laughter, pure and grand,
Two butterflies, in pursuit they soar.

Love is hands entwined, forevermore,
Endless wandering, hand in hand we
explore,
Together, we've trod countless miles,
Through mountains and valleys, love
compiles.

In this very moment, here and now,
Love's the reason, our paths did plow,
Turning pages of poems that inspire,
Our hearts entwined in love's sweet choir.

Love's selfless giving, a radiant ray,
Endless waiting through night and day,
Cotton candy on a street so sweet,
A butterfly clip, a love's heartbeat.

Love's devotion, no holds barred,
For you, my all, forever marred,
Through fire and water, I'll stride by,
In your eyes, my world, I'll imply.

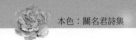

29

片面世界
Perception's Veil

2021 年 4 月

曾幾何時回顧往事
方知那時候的決定
只是片面的認知
造成現在的結果
早已無法挽回

一件事也好
一個人也罷
無論再怎樣努力
也是一道無解的題

不過是陷入片面的漩渦
換個角度看這個世界
也許才會做到全面
難題也不再是難題

萬物都有陰陽面
萬事都存正負心
我看到的是哪一面
你看到的是哪顆心

陰陽太極五行八卦
也許我們眼中的世界
隨著我們意識的昇華改變

多維空間的集合
創造出世界萬物的變化

In moments past, as we reflect with care,

Our choices once made, the paths we dare,

Partial perceptions, decisions from then,
Unveil the present, a tapestry blend,
Lost to time, a chapter laid bare.

A task at hand, or a person's quest,
Striving with might, a challenge's test,
A puzzle unsolvable, enigma's grace,
In a vortex confined, we find our place,
Shift the view, see a world at its best.

Engulfed in swirls of a one-sided stream,
Alter the lens, as if in a dream,
Completeness may flourish, problems relent,
Obstacles dissolve, messages sent,
Dualities dance, in life's grand scheme.

Yin and yang intertwine in the fold,
Positive and negative stories told,
What face do I see, what heart does embrace,
Yours and mine, in this cosmic space,
A universe shaped by perceptions untold.

Tai Chi's balance, five elements in stride,
Consciousness elevates, worlds coincide,
Through ascension of thought, realities rearrange,
In multidimensional embrace, we exchange,
A symphony of existence, where truths collide.

Within dimensions converged, a cosmic art,
Variety's brushstrokes, creating each part,
From the fusion of realms, a symphony played,
Evolving the world, in light and shade,
A dance of creation, where every soul imparts.

30

聖靈雪女王
Queen of the Spirit Snow

2021 年 4 月 28 日 01:51

羽化的霓裳
蝶翅的華髮
彩霞的雲釵
流雲的錦帶

千年的沉睡即將醒來
靈悅的冰晶唱響高歌
異界動盪九州敬仰
輕喚著你的名字
聖靈的女王

快快醒來吧
快快醒來
雪花的旋轉和著
靈曲的節拍

冰峰的傾訴
冰谷陣陣迴響
輕喚著你的名字
聖靈的女王

快快醒來吧
快快醒來

靈媚的雙眼正在

緩緩的睜開

群山震盪
百獸朝拜
彩霞滿天
精靈歌唱

聖靈的女王
揮舞著雲彩的衣袖
號令雪國的子民

降臨福壽安康
擊退外敵
庇護千年平安
子民歡呼雀躍
朝拜聖靈的女王

In the realm where dreams take flight,
In garments woven from starlight,
With butterfly's wings of grace,
And cloud-adorned jewels embrace.

A slumber deep, a thousand years' dream,
Crystal whispers in melodies gleam,
Realms entwine, in cosmic dance,
Whispering your name, a mesmerizing
trance,
Oh Ethereal Queen, in radiant stream.

Awaken, awaken, the dawn's embrace,
Snowflakes pirouette in celestial space,
Harmony of spirits, a symphony's beat,
Echoing through time, a rhythmic feat,
Whispering your name, realms interlace.

Rise, O Queen, from your slumber's veil,
Enchanting gaze, like a celestial sail,
Mountains bow, nature's reverence
shown,
Creatures kneel, your presence known,
Rainbows weave, in skies unveiled.

A sovereign of skies, in splendor adorned,
Guiding the lost, where destinies are
formed,
Bestowing blessings, life's tapestry
weaves,
Guardian of peace, as the land believes,
A thousand years' grace, the realm
adorned,
Hearts uplifted, by your spirit warmed,
Homage to the Queen, voices raised.

31

血色皇冠

Crimson Crown

2021 年 3 月 16 日

古今中外歷朝歷代
血雨腥風屍橫遍野
爾虞我詐詭計多端
骨肉至親毫不留情

機關算盡青史留名
前赴後繼動盪不安
戴上血色的皇冠
決戰千里城邊

臣服於權力的腳下
危機湧於八方
何時才是盡頭
沾了血的皇冠
發著金色的光
加冕無盡的貪婪

得民心者安於天下
失民意者大浪淘沙
千年沉浮
萬載動盪
手握萬里江山圖
哀嘆一將功成
萬骨無名
歷史的車輪壓碎
數代的血色皇冠

Through ages past, from East to West,
Bloodshed and horror, a gruesome test,
Deceit and schemes, a cunning play,
Even kin's affection, they betray.

Machinations unfold, history's tale,
Successors rise, as dynasties trail,
A crimson crown adorns their head,
A thousand miles, where battles spread.

In the annals of time, stories told,
Of empires risen, and those that fold,
A tapestry woven with ambition's thread,
Blood-stained crowns, on the path they
tread.

Bowing to power's weighty might,
Crisis surrounds from every height,
When will the turmoil find its end?
A bloodied crown, its gleam to blend,
Golden radiance, greed takes flight.

Those who win hearts, hold the realm's
key,
Lost in the tide, like grains of sand free,
Centuries' ebb and flow, a restless sea,
A map of vast land held by decree.

One's triumph achieved, yet nameless
bones,
Crushed by the wheel that history owns,
Generations' blood-stained crowns it
shatters,
A tale of power, ambition, and matters.

32

我可以

I Can

慌亂的眼神
亂跳的心
說不出的話語
組織不清思緒
不停的踱腳步轉圈
我要怎樣才能安靜下來

看著遠處的山川
望著擁擠的人群
聽著遠處的鳥鳴
感受著陣陣微風

深深的大口呼吸
靜靜地閉上眼睛
聽著心臟的跳動
調整著有序的思緒
重新整理一個個難題
逐一解決一個個困難

我可以解決
我可以勝任
我可以處理好
我可以做的很好
我可以戰勝一切困難

是的，——我可以！

Eyes in disarray, a frantic glance,
Heart beats wild in a rhythmic dance,
Words unspoken, thoughts astray,
In a whirlwind of steps, I sway.

How can I find tranquility's grace?
Amid distant hills, I fix my gaze,
Crowds bustling, a vibrant stream,
Distant birds' songs, like a dream.

Inhale deeply, let the breath unwind,
Close my eyes, a calm to find,
Hear my heart's rhythm, steady and true,
Organizing thoughts, a task to pursue.

Sorting puzzles, one by one,
Facing challenges, until they're done,
I possess the strength to mend,
To overcome and rise, my journey's end.

I have the power to overcome,
To shine brightly under any sun,
To conquer, achieve, and rise above,
Yes, I can, with strength and love.

Indeed, —— I can!

33

美麗的歌唱
Enchanting Melodies

2021 年 4 月 8 日

我所有的美好都來源於你
陪我度過漫長又孤獨的夜

無論高音還是低音
無論唱的是什麼意境

雨中有你陪我漫步海邊
晴朗你陪我踱步山間

泉水應著你的跳躍
鳥兒唱著我們的並肩

歡笑中你看著我的笑臉
悲傷中你拂去我的淚痕

無論明天會到來什麼
我都不會在畏懼

我有你的陪伴都不再孤單
帶我翱翔音樂的海洋
穿梭於浩瀚的宇宙之間
歌唱出最美的音符

像銅鈴掛在樹間
像泉水叮咚山川
唱出心靈的呼喚
唱出萬物的美好

我要大聲的歌唱
唱出心中的摯愛
唱出真心的感恩
唱出思念的情懷
無論春秋冬夏
唱出萬古常青

All my beauty finds its source in you,
Through the long, lonely nights, you
shine through.

High notes or low, melodies entwine,
No matter the mood, your presence
aligns.

In rain, you stroll with me by the shore,
Under clear skies, to mountains we
explore.

The springs dance to your joyful leap,
Birds sing in harmony as memories seep.

In laughter, you watch my smile unfold,
In sorrow, you wipe away tears untold.

No matter what tomorrow may hold,
Fear shall not take its grip, I'm bold.

With you, solitude has found its end,
Guiding me through music's vast blend,
Navigating the cosmic expanse,
We sing the notes of the grand dance.

Like wind chimes sway in the trees,
Like springs' melody in mountains' ease,
We sing the call of the soul's desire,
Echoing beauty, higher and higher.

I'll sing with a voice unchained,
Love's melody forever sustained,
With gratitude and heartfelt grace,
I sing of longing's embrace.

Through spring, winter, summer, and
fall,
Singing a timeless echo, enthralling all.

34

平凡英雄
Ordinary Heroes

童年的回憶仿佛昨日
美麗的星辰連接著海洋
一直尋找著生命的真諦
希望成為心目中的英雄

可現實中的一幕一幕
敲碎了多數人的美夢
什麼才是真正的英雄

活著的每一天都是英雄

無論是一筆一劃寫在黑板上的字
無論是一橫一豎掃淨馬路上的落
　　葉
無論是一家一戶送的訂單外賣
無論是一左一右指揮著交通
我們都是平凡英雄

在生命的歷程中揮灑汗水
在平凡的點滴中演繹者偉大
啊，平凡英雄
不用在意異樣的眼光
你就是星辰中最耀眼的那顆星

Childhood memories, like yesterday's
dream,
Starry skies connecting oceans' gleam,
In search of life's essence, a quest to
redeem,
Hoping to be the hero, as it may seem.

But reality unfolds in its own way,

Shattering dreams, the sun turns to gray,
What truly makes a hero, they say?

Every day we live is a heroic display.

Be it strokes of chalk on the blackboard's
face,
Or sweeping leaves from a roadside's
grace,
Delivering orders to each home's space,
Guiding traffic with a composed pace,

We are the unsung heroes, humble and
true,
In life's journey, we shed sweat anew,
In the ordinary, greatness we construe,
Oh, ordinary heroes, it's you who shine
through.

Ignore the odd glances, let them fall,
You're the brightest star, outshining them
all,
In the constellation of life's endless
sprawl,
Ordinary hero, you stand tall.

35

意義

Meaning

2021 年 5 月 2 日

回頭看過去的十年
悲歡離合五味雜陳
追求著美好的生活
追逐著心中的執念

突然有一天一切都變了
所有一切歸為零點
那時才幡然醒悟
過去的人生毫無意義
悲傷至極　無法呼吸

一時的迷茫找不到方向
開始懷疑什麼是對
開始領悟什麼是錯
閉上眼睛問問自己

我想成為怎樣的我
我想要過什麼樣的生活
打破我內心所有的局限
重新定義生活的意義

我在世界之中
世界在我心中
成敗翻雲覆雨
悲歡山頂雲端

我意始於原點
我念彈指揮間

存在既有八面玲瓏
意在選擇哪一個面
與我朝夕相伴

指引我如何選擇
傾聽內心的聲音
體會生命的意義

What version of myself do I seek?
What life's image do I wish to speak?
Breaking down limits, I shall not be
weak,
Redefining life's purpose, a journey
unique.

Looking back upon the past ten years'
flight,
A medley of emotions, both dark and
bright,
Chasing after a life so pure and right,
Pursuing dreams with unwavering might.

In this vast world, I do reside,
Within my heart, the world does confide,
Triumph and failure, like a tide,
Mountains of emotions, no place to hide.

Then one day, the world took a twist,
Reduced it all to a starting mist,
Awakening a truth, so hard to resist,
The past held no meaning, it ceased to
exist,
Grief held its grip, a breathless tryst.

From a starting point, my intentions
begin,
My thoughts weave the tale, chapter and
spin,
In every corner, life's facets win,
Choosing a face, where do I fit in?

Lost in confusion, a path unclear,
Doubting what's right, what's dear,
Unraveling truths once held near,
With closed eyes, I pondered, clear.

Guided by my heart's own plea,
Listening within, my soul's decree,
Embracing life's essence, pure and free,

36

追求完美
Pursuit of Perfection

從幻想的美好回到殘酷現實
怎麼還會相信這是一個完美世界

每天都活在不完美中
面對各種不公平
該如何平復委屈的心情
面對各種不應該
將怎樣去解決

也許是要求不同
也許是條件不同
完美的定義凝重

或許是時代進步
推著我們的腳步
也許是藝術和昇華
讓我們創造更多的完美
保持進取的心
迎接下一個完美和不完美

也許太多追求極致
也許太多故事都太完美
也許現實與理想的差距太大
我們越來越感覺到不完美的事太
多

當故事的結局出乎意料
當現實的枷鎖附在自身

Perhaps diverse desires in every heart
reside,
Conditions divergent, paths chosen with
pride,

Perfection's essence, profound and
refined,
A weighty definition, in every mind
entwined.

Striving for excellence, a relentless quest,
In the pursuit of utmost, we aim to
impress,
Yet tales spun seamlessly, a world of
make-believe,
Too perfect to be true, reality we
misconceive.

The chasm 'twixt dreams and life's stark
embrace,
Shackles of the ordinary, tightly in place,
From idyllic fantasies to harsh truths we
yield,
Can this be a world, where perfection is
concealed?

In a realm of imperfections, we navigate
the day,
Confronting inequalities that come our
way,

How to mend the heart, soothe the
grievous ache,
In the face of injustices, what path to
undertake?

Perhaps it's an era advancing us ahead,
Guiding our steps, where progress is
spread,
Or the realm of art, where souls interlace,
Creating more perfection, in each
boundless space.

With hearts full of ambition, forever to
aspire,
Greeting the spectrum, where perfections
and flaws conspire,
With unwavering spirit, we embrace the
quest,
To welcome the next perfect, and
imperfect, with zest.

37

前塵
Echoes of the Past

如果說有來生
如果說有前世
我會生在什麼年代
也許騎著馬跨著弓
飛馳在茫茫的草原
牛羊成群如白雲點點

也許會成為一顆種子
飛入山澗之間
落入石縫中長成參天大樹
風吹雨打堅韌不拔

也許我是一隻雄鷹
翱翔在九霄之上
盤旋於群山之間
朔目望著這世界萬物
芸芸眾生

也許我是一隻螻蟻
在黑暗中穿梭爬行
牢記自己的使命
保衛族群的安寧
捍衛帝王之城

也許我們的靈魂
經歷過千百次洗禮
才成為今天的我
才成為今天的你
善良無畏
勇敢真誠

也許是我們前世的千百次擦肩
換來今世我能站在你的面前

If there were lives beyond, a tale to be
spun,
And pasts unseen, before this one,
In which era would my soul find its way,
Perhaps riding steeds, bow in hand,
Across endless grasslands, a wild, open
land,
Where herds dot the landscape like
clouds in array.

Or a seed, to a mountain's embrace I'd
soar,
Settling in crevices, a giant to explore,
Resilient 'gainst elements, unwavering,
pure.

Mayhaps an eagle, to the heavens ascend,
Above mountain peaks, my flight never
end,
With keen eyes, I'd watch o'er, each life
transcend,
Witness to the world, where souls
contend.

Or a simple ant, in shadows I'd roam,
Through darkness and struggles, find a
place to call home,
Duty-bound, I'd guard, protect and
atone,
Defending my kin, my fortress, my own.

Our souls, through ages, have danced and
entwined,
In countless existences, a tapestry
designed,
Destined to meet, souls forever aligned,
In this life's embrace, our spirits combine.

Through the ebb and the flow of time's
ceaseless tide,
We emerge anew, with hearts open wide,
Becoming the heroes, side by side,
Fearless and kind, love our guide.

A history of connections, lives
intertwined,
Through trials and growth, our souls
defined,

A story of love, both gentle and kind,
In this grand cycle, our spirits aligned.

So let our souls journey, once more, once
again,
In the dance of existence, let love be our
reign,
Two souls united, breaking every chain,
In the grand symphony of life, we remain.

38

外星人之旅
Odyssey of the Extraterrestrial

駕著飛船探險
來到了地球之星
這迷人的藍色星球
這夢幻的白色雲團
下潛低飛卻看到
吃驚的景象

煙霧迷漫
黑氣繚繞
污染重重
垃圾添海

弱肉強食
武力爭端

難道地球開啟了
自我毀滅程序

驚恐萬分
迅速返航

原來這奇幻的美麗下隱藏著
各種自我傷害

要怎樣才能拯救這顆美麗的星球
保留下宇宙中這奇跡般的美好

Mist veils, dark clouds entwine,
Pollution's grip, oceans' decline,
Trash-filled seas, conflicts align,
Earth's self-destruction, signs malign.

Fear grips as truth unfurls,
Swift return, away from whirls,
Beneath enchantment, harm swirls,
Hearts ache for a world that hurls.

To save this beauty, unite we must,
Preserve the wonder, in cosmic trust,
Mend the wounds, let love adjust,
For a starlit future, in goodness thrust.

In ship's embrace, to Earth I soar,
A blue gem, clouds adore,
Descending low, sights abhor,
Shocking scenes forevermore.

39

一千年以後
A Thousand Years Beyond

我從夢中醒來
在一千年以後的星球
人類實現了永生
農作物機器自動化生產
物資豐富
應有盡有

人們無需勞動工作
進入高級生命階段
實現人機共體
所有信息共享

所有資訊想到即可得到

我在 @898 星球上
人類找到數以千個可以生活的星
球
在各個星球之間旅行

在這裡沒有痛苦
沒有饑餓寒冷
沒有貧窮不安
沒有生存壓力

我和家人住在水下
藍色水城之中
看著五光十色的魚
自由自在水中游來游去
講著幾百年前的星球趣事
同我一千歲的小狗在空中之城玩
耍
真是太嚮往的時刻了

Awakened from slumber's embrace,
In a world a thousand years' trace,
Humanity bathed in ageless light,
Eternal life, a celestial flight.

Crops tended by mechanized hand,
Abundant resources blanket the land,
No toil remains, no labor's weight,
A realm of harmony, shared fate.

Transcending realms, life's ascent,
Human and machine, a bond intent,
All knowledge shared, a cosmic dance,
In unity, existence's expanse.

@Planet898, a beacon afar,
Countless stars, life's avatar,
Exploring worlds, a cosmic tide,
Thousand vistas to roam, to ride.

No agony, no hunger's toll,
Chilled winds and want, no more,
An era devoid of struggle and strife,
In underwater realms, a serene life.

Amidst the azure water's embrace,
Family dwells in a watery space,
Gaze upon fish in myriad hues,
Unrestrained, as life they peruse.

In stories told of yore's distant hold,
A playful dog, a companion bold,
Amongst the city in the sky's lofty sprawl,
Yearned moments, dreams enthrall.

40

半生緣
Half a Lifetime's Bond

2022 年 2 月 9 日

愛恨離　空山隱盡　空悲切
半生盡　愛恨情仇　歎奈何
餘生緣　止在朝夕　雲海間
永相忘　笑看銀河　渡忘川

回頭看　人生漫漫　盡蹉跎
低下頭　哀思漫天　半疑惑
玲瓏心　不盡漫步　淚先流
苦亦苦　來來回回　是盡頭
甜中甜　你濃我濃　白首現

仰天笑　真真假假　何盡無
空望穿　世間繁華　何盡有
餘生念　何去何從　互相望
來生緣　朝朝暮暮　誓不棄

Turning back, life's path untold,
Moments squandered, stories unfold,
Bowing low, grief fills the sky,
Half-doubting thoughts, reasons why.

Heart like jade, wandering free,
Tears fall first, a poignant sea,
Bitter, oh bitter, cycles spin,
Sweet as honey, love we're in.

Gazing skyward, laughter's blend,
True and false, to no end,
Yearning pierced, world's array,
Endless choices, night and day.

In the years ahead, thoughts abound,
Where to go, what can be found,

Futures entwined, day and night,
Promises whispered, never slight.

Love and hate, fade from view,
Vanishing into the misty hue,
Half a life, passions bittersweet,
Sighs of "what if" repeat.

Remaining days, in morning's glow,
Bound by fate, as time does flow,
Forgotten forever, laughter fills the sky,
Across the Milky Way, spirits shall fly.

41

中子定律
Neutron Law

你的雙眼
前世今生浮現
抬起頭望著宇宙太空
星球旋轉爆裂又重生

時空停止在來去空間
沉浮過往不見
前天昨天今天
錯過的時間

分子中子媒介
旋轉的定律空間

空氣溫度濕度
宇宙中沒有溫度

奇跡中的奇跡
創造今天你我

紅色的光環
閃爍著美麗的光芒
點點滴滴中
凝聚成碩大天體

億萬年的火焰
燃不盡的流光
見之所見
並非真實所見

周而復始
世間萬物循環
當我再睜開雙眼
時間停止不前

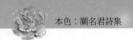

每個細胞凝固
停在斷層空間

Flames of eons, a burning fire,
Endless light, a ceaseless choir,
What's seen may not be real,
Cycles turning, life's grand wheel.

Your twin eyes, a glimpse of lives past,
Lift your gaze to cosmic vast,
Planets swirling, bursting, reborn,
In time's embrace, all else torn.

Ever onward, the world spins 'round,
Nature's rhythm, its sacred sound,
As you open your eyes once more,
Time stands still, as in days of yore.

Moments cease in the ebb and flow,
Yesterday, today, to and fro,
Lost in the space of missed chance,
Time's dance, a cosmic trance.

Each cell solidifies, transcends,
In rifts of space, life suspends.

Particles, neutrons weave,
Laws of rotation, space they cleave,
Temperature, humidity in air,
Void of warmth in cosmic lair.

Miracle within miracles do form,
Crafting today, where hearts are warm,
Halo of red, a luminous grace,
Glistening dots in boundless space.

42

年齡
Timeless Heart

一開始我聽到的
看到的　都告訴我
年齡不重要
愛情第一重要

直到後來我才發現
這世間唯一不能改變的
也許就是年齡了

胖瘦可以改變
美醜可以改變
善良可以改變

天真可以改變
財富可以改變
貧窮可以改變

唯一不能改變的
就是我的過往

經歷的風霜雨雪
天寒地凍春去秋來
一天天增加的年紀
早已事過境遷
物是人非

但是
心中的熱情還在
心中的希望還在

我還是從前的我
又不是從前的我

當一切隨時間改變
也許只有我的心沒有改變

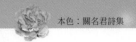

滿臉的熱情依舊
真誠的等待著你的到來

尋遍千山萬水
踏過山河冰川
來時的路依舊
歸去的心凜然

霞光浮現
你是否還是
那個從前

Shapes may shift, from thin to round,
Beauty's mask, in ways unbound,
Kindness learned, innocence found,
Fortunes grown, from the ground.

All may shift and rearrange,
But one thing won't undergo a change,
My past, my history, my tale,
Carved within like an ancient trail.

Weathered by life's rain and snow,
Spring's departure, autumn's glow,
Years keep adding to my name,
Time's progression, still the same.

Yet amidst this ebb and flow,
Passions burn, their fervor aglow,
Hopes endure, their light does show,
Unwavering, in hearts' tableau.

In the beginning, what I heard,
What I saw, each whispered word,
Age, they said, holds little sway,
Love's the treasure, come what may.

Yet later on, I came to see,
One thing that remains constant, free,
In this world of ever change,
Age, the one unyielding range.

I remain the me of old,
Yet transformed, as stories unfold,
Amidst the shifting sands of time,
My heart's flame continues to climb.

Through mountains, waters, ice and
snow,
Journeying where the wild winds blow,
The road I tread still bears my stride,
Yet my heart, with newfound pride.

In hues of dawn's celestial art,
Do you still embody that early part?
As shadows rise and daylight wanes,
Do you remain, untouched by change?

43

尋你
Seeking You

迷航中前方閃爍的明燈
是我大風大浪的指引
你是我生命中那些無可比擬
縱使前方有狂風暴雨
我身已遍佈傷痕
沒有什麼可以擊退我前行

搖搖晃晃的身體
接過天邊遺落的繁星
明燈閃閃不滅不離
此生只為找到你

翻過排山倒海的巨浪
踏過荊棘遍生的叢林
歲歲年年風雨不懼
只為找到你
人山人海千重幻境
千里萬里只為相聚
縱天下尋盡
此生只為有你

Amidst the lost expanse, a distant light,
Guiding through storms, the darkest
night,
You, unmatched in life's grand array,
In tempests fierce, you lead the way.

Though scars of battles mark my skin,
No force can halt where I begin,
Swaying, stumbling, yet I stand,
Holding the stars from heavens grand.

The beacon shines, unwavering bright,
In ceaseless dance, a steadfast sight,

Through trials vast and oceans wide,
This life's pursuit, to be by your side.

Cresting waves that surge and roar,
Through thorns and thickets, I explore,
Years and seasons, tempest-torn,
Seeking you, forever sworn.

Amidst illusions, realms untold,
Across vast lands, in shadows cold,
Through time and space, my quest holds
true,
For in this life, my aim is you.

Through mountains high and valleys
deep,
In dreams and wakefulness, I leap,
Through every heartache, every thrill,
In this vast world, your love fulfill.

44

我該如何拯救你
How Can I Save You

2022 年 9 月 7 日

黑暗中點點的星光
告訴我黎明就要到來
胸中壓抑的怒火
熊熊燃燒
讓我無法呼吸
無法呼吸
眼中泛著淚光
模糊了世界
一滴一滴落下
落在我心中

我該怎麼辦
用盡全力　快速止血
我該怎樣做
才能挽救你的生命

鮮血又一滴一滴流下
染紅了地面
染紅了海水
你的眼神顫抖著
我的心也顫抖著

寒風中的燈火燦燦
哪一盞燈是為你而點亮
群山峻嶺　巨石巍屹
停止的腳步蹣跚

僵硬的身軀無法前行
我該帶你去向何方
我該怎樣拯救你
我的愛人

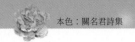

In the dark, a glimmer, starlight's
embrace,
Foretelling dawn's impending grace,
Within my chest, a smoldering ire,
Burning fierce, a consuming fire,
Suffocating, breathless, I remain,
Tears in my eyes, a world's refrain,
Blur the edges of my sight,
One by one, they fall, in the night.

How do I proceed, what shall I do,
To staunch the flow, to rescue you,
With all my might, I strive to mend,
Your life in peril, my heart's true friend.

Drops of crimson, stain the ground,
Dye the seas, a red profound,
Your trembling gaze, a mirror to see,
My heart too trembles, longing to be free.

In the cold wind's glow, lamps ablaze,
Which light is yours, through life's maze,
Mountain peaks, sturdy and tall,
My steps falter, come to a crawl.

Stiffened form, unable to tread,
Where shall I take you, where to be led,
How can I save you, bring you back,
My beloved, my love, a steadfast track.

y

45

愛情奢侈品
Luxury of Love

2022 年 9 月 16 日

每個人都在忙忙碌碌
為了衣食住行
為了經濟基礎
為了英氣豪邁
為了上層建築般的愛情

朝朝暮暮辛苦付出
在第一階段
追趕著第二階段
愛情對於我來說
真是太過奢侈

只能遠遠的看著

不管怎樣努力總是一場空
忙碌半生　心灰意冷
看清世事無常

唯有心中那一束光還在
照亮前行的方向
愛情才是真正的奢侈品
只有真情最是無價

In ceaseless toil, each soul does tread,
For sustenance and roof o'erhead,
Economic realms, ambitions high,
Love's grand architecture, dreams that
fly.

Day and night, in labor's embrace,
Chasing future's elusive grace,
Love, for me, a distant star,
A luxury, seen from afar.

Despite endeavors, efforts vast,
Life's pursuits, they do not last,
Greyed by time's swift-shifting hand,
Worldly truths we come to understand.

Yet within, a beacon's glow remains,
Guiding through life's uncertain lanes,
Love, the truest luxury of all,
In priceless bonds, our spirits enthrall.

46

九世輪迴

Nine Lives of Reincarnation

2022 年 9 月 20 日

仙島孤寂　看人世間
芸芸眾生　愛恨別離
蓮花浮香　遠飄天界
我心已不在　難捨難離

紅塵造化世修人間苦
山川大地浮起塵埃盡
百年時光揮不去一世情緣
嘆我九百年輪迴
尋你九世愛戀

無盡光陰
蓮花烙心間
無懼亦無悔
打破四海結界
只為護你平安歸來

可粉身亦碎骨
只為見你回眸一媚
千江孤寂千江醉
萬重浪現萬重山

轉世輪迴無止盡
踏雪無痕無畏懼
蕩盡忘川鬼魅
腳踏玉劍縱來回
破盡天規戒律

輕舟搖曳花香百味
金光現　菩提念
赴你九世輪迴

In solitude of fairy isle, I gaze upon the
worldly scene,
Countless lives in love and strife, a cycle
bound by fate's routine,
Lotus fragrance drifts afar, to realms
beyond celestial height,
My heart remains, entwined, adrift,
reluctant to take flight.

In mortal coil, existence weaves its
tapestry of pain,
Mountains, rivers, lands unknown,
gather dust and fade again,
Centuries unfold, unbind, yet threads of
love persist,
Nine hundred years of cycles past,
seeking your love, I insist.

Endless sands of time cascade, like lotus
petals in my chest,
Fearless, resolute, I tread, breaking
barriers, I am on a quest,
For your safe return, I pledge my all, no
regrets, no retreat,

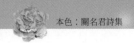
Even if my form crumbles, bones break,
to catch a glimpse so sweet.

A thousand rivers, a thousand
intoxications, I wander through,
Waves upon waves, mountains vast, in
their midst, I find you,
Endless cycles of rebirth, an eternal
dance, never ceased,
Traverse the snowy paths untamed, no
fear, no shadows unleashed.

Ghosts of the River of Forgetfulness, I
banish from my sight,
On a jade sword, I stand and fight,
challenging the rules of day and night,
A vessel sails, fragrant blooms, a myriad
of flavors near,
Golden radiance reveals the path, Bodhi
whispers calm and clear.

Across your nine lives' reincarnations, I
vow to remain,
In this poetic saga of love, transcending
time's earthly chain.

47

使命
Calling of Purpose

2022 年 10 月 3 日

一顆種子落在懸崖
艷日高照　風吹雨打
小小種子發了芽
可它有點怕
腳下萬丈深淵
岩石峭壁
沒有泥土適合紮根
我該怎樣才能長大

嫩芽在深夜的寒風中顫抖
清晨的朝露滋潤著它

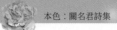

親吻著它小小的臉頰
溫暖的晨輝仿佛是金色的外衣
緊緊的包裹著弱小的身體

心底的使命推著它紮根岩石
現在沒有什麼能阻擋它的成長
依著峭壁慢慢長成一顆樹
開著白色的花
結出金色的果

顆顆種子隨風飄散
四海為家
繼續完成它們的使命
是生命的勳章
一往無前
永不退縮

A seed descends upon a cliff's harsh edge,
Bathed in sun's brilliance, winds' fervent
pledge,
Tiny sprout emerges, timid, yet bold,
At abyss's brink, where stories are told.

Perched above a chasm's daunting maw,
Rugged rocks, unyielding, fill its raw,
No nurturing soil, no bed for its roots,
How shall it thrive amid life's pursuits?

Trembling 'neath the midnight's icy
breeze,
Morning dew's caress, like tender keys,
Kisses its cheeks, a golden attire,
A dawn's embrace, a warming fire.

Deep within, a mission drives its core,
Against all odds, to root and explore,
No force can hinder, no obstacle remain,
A tree on the precipice, breaking the
chain.

Blossoms of ivory grace, on limbs they
dance,
Golden fruits emerge, a tale of chance,
Seeds carried by winds, to distant shores,
In quest of purpose, life's emblem it
stores.

Undaunted, it marches, a steadfast creed,
Through all adversity, it shall succeed,
A symbol of valor, unwavering might,
For in this story, resilience takes flight.

48

遲來的初戀
Belated First Love

第一次感覺到淚如雨下
止都止不住的心疼
不停的顫抖　呼吸急促
胸口仿佛千斤巨石
壓的無法呼吸
慢慢的　反復出現
一幕一幕畫面
不夠好　不應該

為什麼會出現
又為什麼會消失
默默地低下頭

縮成一團

包裹著，一層又一層

沒有光，沒有聲

沒有空氣　沒有力氣

沒有一切

又是一陣心疼

如潮水一般

我打開包裹著我的一切

看著光，聽著街上的雜亂

呼吸著

大口呼吸著

尋找各種顏色

讓我開心的顏色

那種遲來的感受終於來了

漸漸的，我笑了

傻傻的笑

原來是我錯了

罷了，就讓這滴淚

結束這遲來的一切

迎接下一個嶄新的黎明

First time tears fell like rain,

Heartache unrestrained, a piercing pain,

Trembling relentlessly, breath held tight,

Chest burdened, as if with endless might.

Slowly, it arrives, scenes replay,

Inadequacy lingers, shadows gray,

"Why not better? Why this way?"

Questions echo, doubts at bay.

Why it appears, then disappears,

Head bowed low, hiding fears,

Curling inward, layers unfold,

Shrouded in darkness, story untold.

No light, no sound, no air, no might,

Emptiness engulfs, a starless night,

Aches consume, like waves so high,

Unveiling a truth, a silent cry.

Like tides that surge, I reveal my core,
Unwrap the layers, unveil the store,
Bask in the light, street sounds surround,
Inhale deeply, in each breath, I'm found.

Seeking colors, vibrant and bold,
Shades that bring joy, like stories told,
Belated feelings now at play,
Slowly, a smile finds its way

For I realize, my path's not wrong,
Let this teardrop be a song,
End this delayed, uncertain night,
Welcome the dawn with newfound light.

49

反噬
Backlash

從來沒有想到
曾經認為不重要的事
正在一劍一劍
一刀一刀刺在胸口
重重的快要停止呼吸

曾經以為時間很慢很長
盡情揮霍
如今變得又快又短
轉瞬即逝

曾經以為金錢不重要
理想萬歲

現如今日夜奔走
為五斗米折腰
麻木的心
麻木的神智不清

曾經以為一切不重要
感情最重要
全心全意的付出
換來的一句句冰冷的無情加絕情
是我錯了嗎

一顆未變的心
用質疑的目光掃視著探測著
是什麼反噬的咒語
反噬我的人生
難道真的要體驗盡世間的七情八
苦
才能算是完整的人生嗎

我找不到答案
什麼才是正確的方向
正確的路

不要忽視每一個細節
它會從另外一個方向
重新出現在你的面前

Never once did I foresee,
Trivial matters once set free,
Now each thrust, a dagger's art,
Pierces my chest, a heavy heart.

Time, I thought, slow and vast,
Squandered freely, moments cast,
Now fleeting, swift as light,
Moments vanish from my sight.

Money, once deemed less to prize,
Ideals reigned, reaching skies,
Now day and night, I bend and bow,
For mere sustenance, I plow.

Numbness wraps my heart, my mind,
Once unimportant, all left behind,
Emotions spent, met with cold disdain,
Was my pursuit, then, in vain?

An unchanging heart I hold,
With questioning gaze, I behold,
What backlash of curses did ensnare,
To mar my life, to bear and share?

Must I taste life's every hue,
Its bitter and sweet, all its view,
To claim a life full, complete,
Enduring sorrows and joys, replete?

Answers elude my searching soul,
Which path to tread, which life to
unfold,
In every detail, a lesson lays,
From another angle, another phase.

In the tapestry of life's grand design,
No thread too small, each intertwine,
For each detail, in its own way,
Will resurface anew, another day.

50

望著你
Gazing at You

朦朦朧朧睜開雙眼
背影閃閃人已不見
匆匆的腳步已經走遠
還來不及說聲謝謝

尋尋覓覓茫茫人海
二年之後才有了你的消息
最近的航班飛到你的城市
終於再次見到了你的背影
那記憶中的恍恍惚惚
我一直記掛的那個身影
出現在我的面前

望著你
淚水在眼眶打轉
望著你
一張俊俏的臉
望著你
微笑一點一點浮現
望著你
一步一步向我走來

心跳快要停止在此刻
血液一點點沸騰在腦海
尋找了二年的你終於出現

望著你
竟然說不出話來
緊緊的抱著你
久久不願分開

No time for thanks, you slipped like a
star.

Amid the crowd, in the vast sea of faces,
Two years gone by, your message traces,
Recent flights led me to your city's
embrace,
Once again, your silhouette, I chase.

The hazy memory, once distant and dim,
The figure I've cherished, now before me,
within,
Gazing upon you, my eyes brim with
tears,
A handsome face, erasing my fears.

A smile emerges, bit by bit,
Your steps towards me, a heartfelt feat,
My heartbeat falters, near its end,
In my mind, boiling blood ascends.

Two years searching, you reappear,
Gazing at you, words disappear,
Holding you close, tightly entwined,
Reluctant to part, forever confined.

In a misty gaze, my eyes unfold,
Your fading figure, a tale untold,
Hastened steps have wandered afar,

51

護心鱗

Guardian Scale

東海之下的水晶宮
藍色宮殿　悠悠仙氣
巨大的海蚌張開殼
沉睡的公主　美艷無雙

海波輕拂起她藍色的紗裙
海蟹輕敲著助眠的音樂
蝦兵蟹將屹立兩旁
巨大的夜明珠散發明亮的光

公主手中抱著一塊金色的鱗甲
那是西海龍王的護心鱗

送給他最心愛的公主碧瀾

邪族侵犯東海之濱
西海龍王帥兵平亂
百年爭戰　未有歸期
真摯的愛人在日日等待

護心鱗發出金光傳遞捷報
待到愛人凱旋歸來
永生永世　相愛相伴
仙侶愛眷　九天齊歡

Beneath the East Sea's shimmering
expanse,
A crystal palace in a mystical trance,
A palace of blue, an ethereal abode,
A giant clam's embrace, where a princess
lies in repose.

Her gown of azure, caressed by sea's
embrace,

Crabs play a lullaby, a soothing grace,
Shrimp soldiers stand sentinel, steadfast
and bold,
A massive pearl illuminates, a beacon to
behold.

In her arms, a golden scale she holds
tight,
The heart-guarding armor of the Sea
Dragon's might,
A gift from the Sea King, his cherished
pride,
For his beloved princess, by his side.

Intruders of darkness encroach the
Eastern shore,
Sea Dragon King marshals his forces, a
battle to restore,
Centuries of conflict, a war unceasing,
Yet undying love prevails, hearts ever-
reaching.

The heart-guarding scale emits a golden
light,

A message of triumph, dispelling the
night,
As the victorious lover returns from the
fray,
Eternal companions, united to stay.

Bound by love's oath, forever entwined,
Celestial lovers, their hearts combined,
When celestial fatigue calls for their rest,
In the Ninth Heaven's embrace, they find
joy's crest.

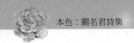

5²

上層建築

Superstructure

2023 年 1 月 23 日

我們每天都在忙碌著
不停於是是非非
糾結於半斤八兩
痛苦於成功失敗
迷茫於大城小愛

日出而做日落而息
風霜雨雪腳步不停
人生百態周而復始
不停尋找的真諦名言

渴望有一個靈魂伴侶
在生活的無奈中取捨
抬頭望著天空的日月星辰
解不開生命的意義真諦

渴望的未來在不確定的方向
積累成雄偉的上層建築
映在心中成不朽的豐碑
刻上幸福美好的人生體驗

In ceaseless haste, our days unfold,
Caught in the turmoil of truths untold,
Entangled in matters great and small,
Tormented by victories and failures that
befall.

From sunrise to sunset, we persist,
Through winds and rains, our steps insist,
Life's myriad hues, an eternal dance,
Seeking the essence, truth's exalted
trance.

Yearning for a soulmate to share life's
stride,
Navigating choices, in circumstance's
tide,
Gazing at the skies, sun, moon, and star,
Yet the meaning of life remains afar.

The future we long for, an uncertain
quest,
A towering structure, in time's endless
test,
Engraved in our hearts, a monument
grand,
Carved with joys and experiences, life's
sacred land.

53

幸運
Fortunate Blessings

漸漸才發現自己有多幸運
成長在一個平凡的家庭
沒有血雨腥風陰謀算計
只有溫馨甜蜜平靜平常

長在一個和平年代
沒有戰亂紛爭
只有幸福的車水馬龍
朝九晚五

長在一個有山有水
有雪有霧淞的美麗城市

春有漫天繁花
冬有萬里雪飄

長在一個好的時代
見證衛星升空
體驗過電車高速馳騁

長在一個恒溫的星球上
沒有烈焰的十個太陽
沒有冰冷的十個月亮
越來越珍惜每一個日出日落
靜靜地感受每一次呼吸的甘甜
每喝一口水都是幸福

越來越愛這個藍色的星球
願你永遠伴隨著依賴你的芸芸眾
生
生命有你才是最幸運的延續
每天看到太陽準時升起
都很幸運了

Gradually, I realize my fortune's embrace,
Nurtured in a home of simple grace,
No bloodshed's storm, no plots entwine,
Just warmth, sweetness, a tranquil line.

Born into an era of tranquil peace,
No wars, no strife, only joy's increase,
Days filled with the hum of mundane
ways,
Nine-to-five rhythms, life's gentle phase.

In a city with mountains and rivers
abound,
Snowflakes and mist, a beauty unbound,
Spring's blossoms paint the skies above,
Winter's snowfall, a blanket of love.

In an age of progress, I have my place,
Witnessing satellites' ascent in space,
Speeding on trams along the track,
A world of wonders in my grasp.

On a planet where temperatures hold,
No scorching suns, no icy cold,

Cherishing each sunrise and its glow,
Breathing sweet, in each moment's flow.

Growing fond of this blue sphere's light,
May you forever guide souls through the
night,
Life's continuum, blessed by your care,
With each rising sun, our joys we share.

Indeed, with every dawn that's seen,
A sense of luck, a tranquil dream.

54

宇宙之光
Cosmic Luminescence

遙遠之外的星球上
住著我們的願望
對我們微笑的眨眼
為我們指引前進的方向
千萬顆願望匯成銀河
那是最美的宇宙之光

歷經世代的時光蹉跎
不斷的孕育新生命
延續著希望之光

那是生命之光
到達心靈的彼岸
點燃新的希望
再多的險阻也不會退縮
呈現出耀眼奪目的色彩
那是我們心中的光

永不熄滅的——
宇宙之光

The light of life, a beacon true,
Transcends the depths, emerges anew,
Igniting hope, a flame so bold,
No obstacle can make it fold.

Radiant hues, a dazzling sight,
Within our hearts, a guiding light,
Unquenchable, it forever gleams,
The cosmic light of boundless dreams.

Upon a distant star's embrace,
Our wishes dwell, a sacred space,
Blinking eyes that smile so bright,
Guiding us through day and night.

Countless dreams, a galaxy's array,
The universe aglow in astral ballet,
Across epochs, time's flowing stream,
Nurturing new life, like a cherished
dream.

55

好無奈
Unyielding Surrender

面對生活的總總壓力
真是有點喘不過氣了
每天睜開雙眼
望著初升的紅日
有一些溫暖的內心
得到些許安慰

城市的車水馬龍
哪一刻為誰停留過
萬家燈火闌珊處
哪一處的燈為我點亮著

有時拼盡全力
還是無能為力
也許這就是人生百態吧

啊　真的好無奈

明天的朝陽會又一次升起
再次溫暖每一個人的內心

也許　這就是生活
是的　這就是生活

Amid life's pressures, a struggle to
breathe,
Each day, I wake, my soul to retrieve,
Gazing at the rising sun so red,
A hint of solace in its warmth
widespread.

Within, a flicker of warmth resides,
In its gentle embrace, my heart abides,

Through city's hustle, a river's flow,
For whom did time pause, lights aglow?

In the glow of countless city lights,
Which one guides me through my nights?
Amid the sea of faces, a bustling tide,
Whose light is there to be my guide?

Sometimes I strive with all my might,
Yet still, I'm caught in an endless fight,
Perhaps this is life's diverse array,
A journey through shadows and sun's ray.

Ah, a feeling of helplessness lingers on,
Yet tomorrow's sunrise, a new dawn,
Warming the hearts of every soul,
This is life's rhythm, its ever-changing
role.

Maybe this is life, in all its grace,
A tapestry woven in time and space,
Yes, this is life, with its highs and lows,
A symphony of emotions, as it flows.

56

向陽而生

Blossoming Toward the Sun

漫長的黑夜不是盡頭
寒冷的冬季終將過去
即使再苦再難
也從不放棄
你的心中有一盞明燈
指引走向正確的道路
永不迷失前進的方向

終有一天光明會到來
掃盡黑夜溫暖萬物
生生不息

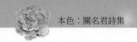

本色：關名君詩集

向陽而生

浮雲散去

虹光漫天

笑容浮現在每一個純真的臉上

清澈善良

不卑不亢

包容一切的涵養於世

閃耀的靈魂永遠相伴

豪邁的樂聲震撼山谷

整齊的腳步踏向征程

我們一起攜手

向陽而生

The endless night is not the end,
Cold winter's grasp, it will transcend,
Though bitter trials, hardships persist,
In never yielding, we persist.

Within your heart, a guiding light,
Leading to paths that are just and right,

Never lost, we forge ahead,
Onward, where the light is spread.

A day will come when brightness gleams,
Banishing darkness, fulfilling dreams,
Life's eternal pulse, it beats and thrives,
Emerging strong as daylight arrives.

Clouds disperse, revealing a rainbow's
grace,
Smiles emerge on each innocent face,
Pure and kind, a gentle refrain,
Embracing all, free from disdain.

With a spirit radiant, forever near,
Resounding laughter through valleys
clear,
Unified steps, a purpose in stride,
Together, we rise, side by side.

In unity's embrace, under the sun,
Our journey unfolds, as one,
Towards the light, we strive anew,
For in unity, strength and hope accrue.

140

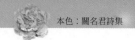

57

異鄉人
Wanderer's Reverie

離開從小生活的地方
獨自一人來到遙遠的城市
有些不捨和欣喜
有些孤獨和迷茫

忙於生活和工作
忙於適應和感受
格外的思念親人和故鄉
份外覺得自己的渺小
這城市的繁華
每一個在異鄉的人啊
好像有很多的朋友
又好像一個也沒有

好像每天都忙忙碌碌
又好像還在原地踏步
當有了第二和第三故鄉
更想念出生的地方

大江南北
縱橫萬里
心早已飛回
那兒時的秋千
小夥伴的嬉戲聲中

林間的蟲飛鳥鳴
山泉溪間捕魚捉蝦
童真志趣
呼喚你的名字

那個在夢中
出現千百次的畫面
獨在異鄉唯意境
月晴圓缺故鄉明

Leaving the place I've known since youth,
Alone I tread to a distant truth,
Mixed emotions, reluctant yet glad,
Lonely moments, lost and somewhat sad.

Busy with life, adapting anew,
Navigating feelings, fresh and true,
Yearning for loved ones, home's embrace,
Feeling small in this bustling space.

City's grandeur shines with allure,
Each stranger here, a potential rapport,
Yet amidst the bustle, it seems,
Connections slip like fleeting dreams.

Days go by in a whirlwind race,
Yet stagnation still leaves a trace,
With second and third homes now
defined,
Yearning deepens for the place enshrined.

North and south, rivers wide,
Across the lands, far and wide,
Heart takes flight, nostalgia's call,
To the swings of autumn, voices small.

In the woods, birds take flight,
Streams cascade, fishing day and night,
Childhood's spirit, pure and clear,
Echoes your name in the heart's sphere.

In dreams, you appear countless times,
A painting etched in rhythm's chimes,
In foreign lands, it's where I find,
The moon's phases, hometown's bind.

58

天下生蓮
Lotus Blossoms Across the World

轉眼間五千年時光飛逝
日月長恒　流光飛轉
山草花木　悠長
半夢半醒間
聽到來自千年的誓言
"用我原神換你永生"
縱有萬般悔不能換回你
雲庭深處一抹靈光悠悠
微弱的氣息等待真身

天下生蓮萬物生息
一世情緣來生再續
我願在等千年
喚醒你的靈魂
前世今生　過往歷歷現

撫平眼角的一滴淚
化做玉骨重塑你真身
我願再等千年
喚醒你的靈魂
前世今生　過往歷歷現

雲海浮沉滄桑巨變
凡心易動　真心不變
心繫天下的你
心繫眾生的我
無極歸一　融為一體
你中有我　我中有你
縱觀天下　無限好風光
群星閃耀　浩瀚天地
握緊你雙手暢遊雲海

In the blink of an eye, five thousand years
swiftly passed
The sun and moon endure, time flows in
a flash
Mountains, grass, flowers, and trees stand
timelessly
Between dreams and wakefulness
I hear an oath from a thousand years past
"I trade my spirit for your eternal life"
Countless regrets can't bring you back
In the cloud palace, a faint spirit
glimmers
A fragile breath awaits the true form

The world blooms with lotus, all life
thrives
Our destined love will continue in the
next life
I'm willing to wait a thousand years
To awaken your soul
Past and present vividly appear

Wiping away a tear from the corner of
my eye
Transformed into jade bones to restore
your true form
I am willing to wait another thousand
years
To awaken your soul
Past and present vividly appear

The sea of clouds rises and falls, enduring
vast changes
The mortal heart is fickle, the true heart
remains unchanged
You, who care for the world
And I, who care for all beings
Returning to unity, merging into one
You within me, and I within you
Gazing across the world, boundless
beauty unfolds
Stars shine brightly, the universe vast
Holding your hands, we roam the sea of
clouds

59

畫展
Palette of Reflections

不同主題　不同意境
吸引著好奇　心之嚮往
各種色彩　此起彼伏
靜靜講訴
無聲的故事

經典的眼神
凝望著
來來往往的人群
各種評論
聲聲不停
發表不同的觀點

燈光的倒影
分隔不同的畫作
時而驚艷　時而詼諧
講訴著作者的心聲
充滿無聲的吶喊
春去秋來　時光荏苒

極高極低的反差
光與影的重疊
線條色塊的起伏
不同空間的層次
溫暖與寒冷的交替
笑容和淚水的記錄
相聚和分離
訴說過去和未來

Different themes, different realms they
hold,
Curiosity stirred, hearts unfold,
Colors dance, in vibrant array,
Silently narrating, tales convey.

Classic gazes fixed upon,
Watching crowds come and go anon,
Endless comments, ceaseless streams,
Voices of varied thoughts and dreams.

Lamp's reflections, painting's divide,
Juxtaposing brilliance and whimsy's ride,
Expressions of the artist's heart,
Silent cries, a masterpiece's art.

Spring to autumn, time does wane,
Highs and lows, a stark terrain,
Merging light and shadow's play,
Layers of space in intricate display.

Warmth and chill, they intertwine,
Laughter and tears in record's line,
Gatherings and partings, they unfold,
Past and future, stories told.

60

玲瓏心
Luminous Heart

青青草　綠綠樹
沁著甜甜的芳香
一步步追著蝶舞熒蟲
一聲聲笑意回蕩山谷
一陣陣微風飄起長髮
一縷縷鉤在嫩芽之上

用一顆玲瓏之心
觀察世界
至真至純
至情至愛

打開心靈的窗
讓一縷陽光照進來
溫暖著真心真意
讓月亮的光照進來
朦朦朧朧恬靜淡然
融合星辰大海　無邊無際

用一顆玲瓏之心
善待萬物
美好的時光
伴隨優雅的呼喚
靜待花開
靜待碩果

飛過山川五岳
四海五湖
善良面對
每一個朝朝暮暮

真誠面對每一顆玲瓏心
每一個潮起潮落
迎金光重現　霞光漫天

Emerald grass, verdant trees,
Scented sweet, a fragrant breeze,
Chasing butterflies, fireflies at night,
Laughter's echo, mountains take flight.

Zephyrs dance, hair in the air,
Tender tendrils touch with care,
With a crystal heart, observe the world,
Pure and true, love's flag unfurled.

Open the window of your soul,
Sunlight's warmth, a golden goal,
Moonlight's glow, a tranquil veil,
Blend of stars and sea, a timeless tale.

With a heart so fine, in every way,
Treat the world with love each day,
Embrace the beauty, moments dear,
Wait for blooms, with patience clear.

Soar above mountains, rivers wide,
Across the seas, under skies so wide,
Kindness as your guiding star,
Every dawn and dusk, where you are.

Face each heart with genuine grace,
Tides of life in their embrace,
Welcoming the dawn's golden hue,
Radiant light, skies painted blue.

61

海浪白花
Ocean's Froth

清晨的光透過金色的雲
落在無邊無際的海面
幽遠綿長
伴著汽笛的鳴響
風推著白色的海浪
不斷向前
拍打著岩石
奏起樂章

小小的貝殼
五光十色
在浪花中起舞
旋轉著身軀擠進白沙

魚兒歡快的加入熱舞
海草揮舞著裙擺點頭行禮
顆顆白沙閃著鑽石的光茫
飄飄灑灑好似雪花飛舞

岸上的螃蟹吐著泡泡
像吹著號角　打著節拍
好一場海洋的歡慶盛會
伴隨著浪花的一推一進
一層一疊永不散場
奏響起生命的華麗樂章

Morning light through golden clouds it
streams,
Upon boundless sea, a tranquil dream,
Vast and serene, a world so wide,
Whistle's song, echoes far and wide.

Wind guides white waves, their joyful
play,
Crashing against rocks, in rhythmic
array,

Tiny seashells, colors abound,
Dancing in foam, on sandy ground.

Fish join the dance, a lively ballet,
Seagrass sways and nods, a gracious
display,
Diamond-like sands glisten in the sun,
Drifting like snowflakes, one by one.

Crabs on the shore blow bubbles with
cheer,
As if playing trumpets, their rhythm
clear,
An ocean's celebration grand and bright,
With waves' embrace, a never-ending
delight.

Layers upon layers, never to disband,
A magnificent symphony across the sand,
Life's vivid chapter, a splendid scene,
In the ocean's embrace, forever serene.

62

玫瑰之吻
Rose's Embrace

也許我是一個渴望愛的人
見到路上手牽手走過的一對
會默默的低下頭

看到滿頭白髮的老人相扶相依
會默默祝福無病無痛長久相依

看到骨肉至親分離淚流滿面
會默默祈禱幸福團聚不離不棄

看到咖啡飄起絲絲白霧
會默默的希望有一個愛人一起分
享

朦朧的背影常常出現在夢中
有時分不清是夢境還是現實

在浪漫的玫瑰花園
火紅的花瓣映著太陽的光暈
如癡如醉　如夢如幻
高大的臂膀緊緊相擁

炙熱的紅唇　甜蜜相吻
深邃的雙眸　看不清模樣
一聲聲呼喚著我的名字
朦朧的身影搖曳

只有那陣陣玫瑰花的幽香
縈繞入夢　回味綿長

A seeker of love, perhaps I am,
Witnessing couples, hand in hand,
Quietly bowing my head in grace,
Longing for love's tender embrace.

Silver-haired elders, side by side,
Whispers of blessings, no need to hide,
Wishing them health and timeless
devotion,
A prayer for unending love's motion.

Loved ones part, tears freely stream,
Silent prayers for a united dream,
Hoping for reunions, hearts held strong,
In love's embrace, where we belong.

Coffee's aroma, delicate and pure,
Silent hopes for a love so sure,
Yearning for a partner to share and hold,
In whispers of warmth, love to unfold.

Faint silhouettes, oft in dreams they play,
Reality and reverie, entwine and sway,
In a rose garden of romance's bliss,
Sun's tender kiss, love's eternal tryst.

Crimson petals mirror the sun's embrace,
In a dreamlike dance, hearts find their
place,

Locked in an embrace, like stars above,
Two souls entwined, united in love.

Fiery lips meet in a sweet caress,
Deep eyes, a mystery, emotions confess,
A voice calls my name, echoes and sighs,
A swaying form, beneath moonlit skies.

Amidst the roses' fragrant trail,
A dream's allure, like a fairytale,
A fragrance lingers, a memory's song,
In the realms of slumber, love lingers on.

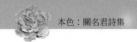

63

你值得擁有美好

Embrace the Beauty
You Deserve

金色晨光灑在身上
溫溫暖暖的味道

清風的親吻好甜
好溫柔是幸福的留戀

盛開的紅色玫瑰
飄著迷人的幽香
茶香四溢　是幸福的美好

林間的清泉　冰涼陣陣
甘甜回味　是幸福的味道

你是這世間的所有美好
真誠　善良　溫柔　美麗

你值得擁有這世間所有的美好
一顆純淨的心面對不平事

你值得擁有世間所有的幸福
春暖花開　心海所開

是的　你值得擁有
這世間所有的美好

Golden morning light upon your skin,
A warmth that whispers from within.

Gentle kisses of the breeze so sweet,
A tender touch, love's bliss complete.

Crimson roses bloom, their scent divine,
A fragrant dance, nature's wine.
Tea's aroma fills the air,
A happiness beyond compare.

In forest glades, a cool spring flows,
Its sweetness in every droplet shows.
You embody beauty, pure and true,
Kindness, grace, in all you do.

You deserve the world's treasures, rare,
A heart so pure, a soul laid bare.
In the face of trials, you stand strong,
A beacon of right amidst the wrong.

You deserve life's joys, happiness untold,
Like spring's embrace, a heart of gold.

Yes, you deserve it all, and more,
Life's beauty knocking at your door.

64

餘生的愛
Love for the Rest of Eternity

我會用餘生去愛你
如果你今生沒有出現
那就是在來生來世
你在等待著與我相逢
我不會有任何遺憾

不知道你是什麼模樣
也不知道你現在何方
但只要你出現在我面前
你就是命中註定的人

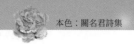

如果你在來生等我
我會含著笑離開這個世界
在平行時空中跟隨你的腳步
堅持你的方向

哪怕你是一顆草
哪怕你是一顆樹
我會靜靜的陪在你的身旁
歷經九世輪迴
再次牽著你的手
微笑看你每一個表情
記著你每一世的模樣

即使你已經忘記了我
並蒂蓮生雙生果
我們餘生的愛戀
永生永世不分離

I'll spend my lifetime loving you,
In this life or the next, it's true.
If not in this present time and space,

In another, we'll meet face to face.

I'll hold no regrets if fate delays,
Unseen your form, in unseen ways.
Yet, when you stand before my eyes,
Destined, our hearts will recognize.

If in another life you wait for me,
I'll depart with a smile, forever free.
Across parallel realms, I'll chase your
stride,
Follow your path, side by side.

Be you a blade of grass, a towering tree,
I'll stand beside you silently.
Through nine lifetimes, a cycle complete,
Once more, our hands in each other's
meet.

Even if your memory of me fades away,
Twin souls, like lotus seeds we lay.
Our love throughout our remaining
years,
Eternal, unending, beyond earthly fears.

65

刻骨銘心的痛
Deeply Etched Pain

原來真正的心疼
是感覺不到痛的
半張著嘴
一個字也說不出來

眼睜睜看著
一眼望穿的世界
淚水一顆一顆
熱熱的成串落下
一顆巨石堵在胸口
停頓呼吸

所有聲音消失
只有心跳的聲音
一聲一聲敲擊著
胸口的巨石
卻聽到了心碎的聲音

時間靜止在此刻
努力的大口呼吸
仿佛吞噬著真實的世界
原來這才是刻骨銘心的痛

像一把把利劍刺進身體
卻無法喊出聲音
天堂和地獄的門在不停交換
已經分不清是黑暗還是光明
原來這才是刻骨銘心的痛

誰來拯救這顆受傷的靈魂
從無限的深淵帶回人間

True heartache, I now understand,
Is pain unfelt, like shifting sand.
Mouth agape, yet no words emerge,
Silent agony, a weighty surge.

Witnessing a world, gazing afar,
Tears descend like fallen star.
Hot, they cascade, a river's flow,
A boulder lodged, breath in tow.

All sounds vanish, silence prevails,
Heartbeats echo, like distant sails.
Each beat pounds against the stone,
A fractured heart's mournful tone.

Time suspended in this sphere,
Gasping for life, the air we shear.
Swallowing reality, a desperate plea,
This, the pain etched, undeniably.

Like daggers thrust into flesh's core,
Voiceless screams, a silent war.
Heaven and hell, doors interchanging,
Darkness or light, forever changing.

Who shall rescue this wounded soul,
From the abyss, to make it whole?
Guided back to humanity's embrace,
From depths profound, find solace and grace.

66

下午茶的幸福
Blissful Afternoon Tea

輕鬆的音樂在耳邊繚繞
陣陣咖啡芳香　清新淡雅
精緻的甜點　酸中帶甜
清掃一切不開心的煩惱

暖暖的陽光灑在身上
無盡的海面　淡淡的藍
輕輕的海風　淡淡的鹹
一天當中最放鬆的時光
盡在下午茶的溫馨快樂

如果時間停止在這一刻
停留住大海的無邊無際
停留住群山的巍屹婀娜
停留住好心情的每一刻
停留住美好青春的腳步

讓時間不再飛逝
陽光再多　些溫暖
清風吹拂我長長的頭髮
讓甜甜的回味綿綿長長

放慢的呼吸
體會時間的悠揚
放慢的心跳
恬靜的望向遠方
珍惜每一刻下午茶的美好時光

Gentle melodies whisper in the ear,

Coffee's aroma, fresh and clear.

Delicate desserts, sweet and tang,

Sweeping away woes with a calming
pang.

Warm sunlight bathes the skin,
Endless sea, hues of blue within.
Gentle ocean breeze, hint of salt,
Most tranquil hours, no thought's tumult.

If time could freeze in this embrace,
Boundless sea and mountains' grace,
Each joyful moment, heart's delight,
Youthful steps and days so bright.

Halt the rushing hands of time,
Let sunlight add warmth to the climb.
Breeze caresses long flowing hair,
Savoring sweetness, beyond compare.

Slow the breath, feel time's gentle sway,
Heartbeat's cadence in a tranquil display.
Gaze to the distance with a calm
embrace,
Cherishing moments, a tea-time grace.

67

居高臨下
A View from Above

在最高的雲層中
結了一層層冰花

團團的雲像厚厚的棉被
蓋在大地上

隨著風飄來飄去
變換著不同的形狀
展示它不同的心情

較黑的雲帶著閃電的怒吼
響徹整個天際

九層天的雲突然間少了很多
輕輕薄薄的停在那一動不動

少了大氣壓的壓迫
呼吸輕鬆了許多
風呼呼的吹著頭髮
寒氣逼人
真有高處不勝寒的意境

夜裡城市燈光相連
燈光星光像一幅連綿的畫卷
星星點點的閃爍

在暗綠色的山脈中
一條條發光的河流像錦帶
相連著五湖四海

與山頂的冰雪輝映
真是一幅美妙的畫卷

In the highest layers of clouds above,
Crystalline ice flowers delicately wove.
Clusters of clouds, like a thick quilt's
embrace,
Blanketing the earth with a gentle grace.

Swaying with the wind, a dance in the
sky,
Shifting forms and shapes as time goes
by,
Displaying different moods, a canvas of
art,
Clouds reveal emotions, from joy to a
heavy heart.

Darker clouds carry lightning's fierce
roar,
Resonating anger, a tempest's uproar.
Nine heavens above, clouds dissipate,
Light and thin, in tranquil state.

Released from the grip of atmospheric
might,
Breathing is easier in this lofty flight,

Whistling winds tousle hair with a
chilling kiss,
Cold air's embrace, a sensation of bliss.

City lights in the night intertwine,
Stars and lamps, in a cosmic design,
A continuous panorama, a flickering
dance,
Sparkling dots of light in a celestial
trance.

Amidst emerald hills, a serene sight,
Rivers aglow like ribbons of light,
Binding lands together with radiant
strands,
Connecting lakes and seas, distant lands.

Atop mountain peaks, snow and ice
gleam,
A wondrous canvas, a vivid dream,
Amidst shadowy green hills, a vivid
display,
A magnificent artwork, nature's bouquet.

68

心之所向
Whispers of the Heart

2022 年 12 月 21 日

我心之所向——遠方
詩情畫意
層巒疊嶂
隱於林中雲海
聽風聞鳥
小泉叮咚
微風拂面
草香徐徐
八方林海
悠悠浮雲腳下
蕩蕩遠方悠揚

心之所向——長空

　　繁星點點

　　無邊無際

　　絮絮如塵

　　縱橫天邊

　　皎潔明月

　　流星劃過天邊

　　閃閃爍爍

　　紅日初映

　　紅月再現

　　紅星閃閃

心之所向——真誠

　　盡心盡力

　　無所畏懼

　　芸芸眾生

　　坦誠相見

　　萬世太平

　　無悔今生

My heart's desire—distant horizons,
A scene of poetic charm, a canvas to be drawn.
Layers of peaks, mountains in a dance,
Concealed in forested clouds, an ethereal expanse.

Listening to winds, the melodies of birds,
A babbling brook's laughter, soft-spoken words.
Gentle breezes caress my face with care,
Whispers of fragrant grass fill the air.

A sea of trees stretches far and wide,
Above, drifting clouds, a captivating ride.
Boundless horizons, a distant serenade,
Echoes of the faraway, an eternal cascade.

My heart's longing—a boundless sky,
Stars twinkling above, a cosmic lullaby.
Endless and vast, like particles of dust,
Across the heavens, they weave and thrust.

A moon, pristine and pure, shines bright,
Streaks of meteors, fleeting trails of light.
Dazzling and sparkling, stars aglow,
A red sun rising, a moon's crimson show.

My heart's pursuit—sincerity's embrace,
Giving my all, without fear's trace.
Facing all beings with an open soul,
A world of harmony, an endless goal.
In this life's tapestry, without regret,
Seeking truth and love, a destiny met.

69

往生門
Gate of Transcendence

在天界與地府之間
有一座互通的往生門
走失的靈魂只要通過此門
就能直達九霄雲殿
亦能直通邪世地府

往生門變換著不同的形狀
時而仙氣繚繞
時而寒氣雷電

什麼樣的靈魂
通向什麼樣的境界

種善因的靈魂
直通九霄雲殿
種惡果的靈魂
下放幽冥地府

每個靈魂手中拿著往生牌
記錄著平生的善因惡果

世代輪迴往返天地之間
善因善果　心懷慈悲善念
往生重生　輪迴再造
生死只在一念之間

Between the realms of heaven and
underworld,
Stands a gateway, a passage untold.
The Bridge to Beyond, connecting
spheres,
Lost souls traverse, shedding earthly
fears.

Shifting in form, this ethereal door,
At times, radiant with heavenly lore,
Others, enveloped in chilling might,
A dance of thunder, an electrifying sight.

What soul you bear dictates the way,
Destinations vary, realms in display.
For virtuous souls, a celestial climb,
To the Cloud Palace, a realm sublime.

Yet souls that reek of malevolent seed,
Descend to realms where shadows lead.
Each clutching a card, life's ledger held,
Recording deeds, tales to be unveiled.

Generations cycle, heaven to earth,
Deeds both tender and of noxious birth.
Kindness sown, compassion's creed,
Leads to rebirth, a transcendent deed.

Life and death converge in thought's
domain,
The Bridge to Beyond, a path to regain.

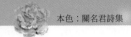

70

看不清的真諦
Obscured Truths

每天都在忙忙碌碌
功名利祿身外之物
每天都在為生活付出

我漸漸看不清楚
金錢名利是經濟基礎
為了愛情的上層建築
唉

看不清呀看不清
想不透呀想不透

忙不完呀忙不完
理還亂呀理還亂

拖著疲憊的身子
看著萬家燈火
什麼才是
正確的答案
周而復始
複雜又簡單

想著明天的太陽
看著今天的月亮
耳邊的鐘聲
遠方的黎明

是是非非終有果
尋尋覓覓不見得
來來往往繁華盡
找找尋尋為一人

哎
看不清啊看不清
聽不見呀聽不見
找不到呀找不到

什麼是對
什麼是錯
思絮雜亂
欲言又止

那個人
那份情
願你
得償所願

Every day in the hustle and bustle,
Chasing after material gains, a struggle.
For livelihood's sake, we toil and strive,
Yet clarity seems to slip, barely alive.

Money and fame, the foundation's creed,
Love's intricate architecture, it breeds.
Oh, the murkiness clouds my sight,
Uncertainty shrouds both day and night.

Can't see, can't grasp, lost in the maze,
Endless busyness, a never-ending craze.
Disarrayed thoughts, tangled and spun,
Seeking answers, one by one.

Dragging weary limbs, I gaze around,
City lights glowing, a bustling sound.
What's the truth, what's the key?
A cycle repeated, complex yet free.

Thinking of tomorrow's sun's embrace,
Watching the moonlight's gentle grace.
The tolling of bells in my ears, I hear,
Distant dawn, it's drawing near.

Right and wrong will find their way,
Yet in seeking, truth may sway.
Through the ebb and flow of life's parade,
Seeking, searching, for just one aid.

Oh, the uncertainty that clouds my
mind,
Deaf to echoes, truth hard to find.
Lost in questions, in this complex land,
What is right? What withstands?

That person, that love, I wish for you,
May your heart's desire come to view.

71

愛戀
Endless Love

風是一種聲音訴說著無盡的相思
雨是一種沉浸表達著各種留戀
光是一種形式代表著愛的顏色
電是一種感覺展示著彼此的心意

願我們的相思
能天長地久
相互理解　相互包容
甜甜的愛是上天的恩賜
茫茫人海中相遇
是無限的幸運

彼此珍惜　相悅相惜
日月星晨
見證著生命的無限美好
山海大川
訴說著海誓山盟

雨雪風霜
讓愛更加堅定不移
櫻花漫天
帶來浪漫無盡

愛戀著你的每一天
是我生命的動力
愛戀著你的每分每秒
組成了我們燦爛的一生
Love you forever

Wind whispers boundless longing,
Rain immerses, fondness belonging.
Light embodies love's embrace,
Electricity conveys hearts' trace.

May our yearning endure,
Mutual understanding, hearts pure.
Sweet love, a gift from above,
In the vast sea of people, we met in love.

Cherishing each other, hearts entwined,
Sun, moon, stars above, they find,
Life's boundless beauty they see,
Mountains, rivers echo vows with glee.

Rain, snow, wind, frost's embrace,
Love steadfast, no trace to efface.
Cherry blossoms, romantic in flight,
Endless allure in petals of white.

Loving you each passing day,
My life's strength, come what may.
Cherishing every moment shared,
Our brilliant journey declared.

Love you forever, evermore,
Boundless devotion, to the core.

72

習慣孤獨
Whispers of Solitude

每一個生命來到世間
都帶著不同的使命
善良包裹著一顆心跳動著
短短長長　無限循環

當每一個生命獨自來到世間
靈魂是孤獨的
生命已經習慣孤獨的存在
人們來去匆匆
表面一片繁華

有很多事情都要獨自去面對

人們選擇彼此照顧
在聚少離多間尋找平衡

我早已習慣了孤獨
即使引來異樣的目光
各種議論紛紛也無妨

只要心中裝著大千世界
從來不會感覺孤單
天下沒有不散的宴席

讓我們一起習慣孤獨
享受每一個獨處的時光
讓自己更加堅強無畏

Each life arrives with a unique call,
Goodness cloaked around, heart's thrall,
Short or long, an infinite loop,
Kindness pulsates, a rhythm to scoop.

As each life enters this worldly plane,

Soul's solitude, a constant refrain,
Accustomed to the solitude we've known,
People come and go, a bustling tone.

Faced with challenges, alone we stride,
Choosing care, in togetherness we
confide,
In the ebb and flow of bonds we weave,
Seeking balance as we believe.

I've embraced solitude's embrace,
Even amid curious gaze and trace,
Whispers of opinions, they can't sway,
A world within, loneliness kept at bay.

With the cosmos held within my heart,
Loneliness is not a counterpart,
For no feast lasts forever in this land,
Let's embrace solitude hand in hand.

Let's find solace in moments alone,
Strength and fearlessness, they've shown,
In solitude's realm, we'll thrive and soar,
Together, embracing it, forevermore.

73

冥王星上的王國
Kingdom on Pluto

深藍色的雲團深處
隱藏著一個冥王星王國
透明中若隱若現的城堡
發光的飛碟快速的移動

高大的藍色發光精靈
揮動著長長的觸角
移動的小房子型的機器
傳輸著能量

地表突現一個巨大的圓形
黑色隱形的裝置升起
向天空吸收圓形的光環

忽然我被傳輸到地下的城堡
紅色的小太陽發出溫暖的光
藍色的小草葉子在抖動變換著形
狀
透明的河流從高處飛落又消失

飛在半空的生物居民歡叫著
仿佛慶祝著盛大的節日
城堡的大門轟隆的打開
飛在半空的列隊整齊排列兩旁

無數的金色小星星灑落在地面
居民歡叫著接星星的能量
巨大的圓形寶座上是他們的國王
全身若隱若現的藍色光芒

轟隆的聲音響徹天宇
我的身體隨著聲波震動
一陣眩暈後眼前一片光明
之前隱形的城堡出現了實體形狀

我融入了居民之中

接到了星星的能量
心情無比的喜悅
我的皮膚變的透明的藍色
紅色的太陽也變成了藍色

我感覺到小太陽給我的能量
消除了饑餓和恐懼感
深深被國王的能量所征服
衷心的臣服聲波的能量之中

Deep within the clusters of sapphire-
hued clouds,
A realm of Pluto's kingdom shrouded in
shrouds,
A translucent castle, elusive to the eye,
Illuminated discs soaring, swift in the
sky.

Towering blue luminescent sprites,
Their tendrils wave, dancing in flights,
Moving houses-like machines transmit,
Energy surging, their essence legit.

Surface reveals a colossal round sphere,
Invisible apparatus, elevates in the air,
Absorbing the halo of celestial light,
Skyward ascent, a mystical sight.

Abruptly I'm transported to the castle
below,
A crimson sun's warmth begins to glow,
Blue blades of grass quiver, shape-shift in
play,
Transparent rivers cascade from heights,
then sway.

Midair denizens rejoice with a cheer,
As if celebrating a grand festival year,
Castle gates boom open, their grandeur
displayed,
In orderly columns, midair they've
arrayed.

Countless golden stars descend from
above,
Residents jubilant, embracing their love,
Upon the grand throne, they honor their
king,

A blue aura cloaks him, an ethereal wing.

Thunderous echoes resound through the
skies,
My being trembles with vibrational ties,
A wave of dizziness, then light emerges,
The once-hidden castle now solidly
surges.

Amongst the residents, I seamlessly
blend,
Harvesting starlight, my essence ascend,
Exultant joy fills my heart's deepest core,
My skin turns translucent blue, evermore.

The red sun's energy flows into me,
Banishing hunger and fear, I'm set free,
Subdued by the king's commanding
might,
Submissive to sound waves, in tranquil
light.

74

空．另一個我

Echoes of the Empty Self

2023 年 5 月 26 日

如今的我幾經磨難
痛苦艱辛
兜兜轉轉日日忙碌
心裡更加迷茫

我一直再尋找
生活的真諦
所見所聞所感所悟
卻越來越迷茫空蕩

一直忙碌的我
到底為了什麼
為了多存一些積蓄？
為了買名牌名表名車？
為了房子更大一些更舒適美觀？
為了更多人認識我　瞭解我　欣
賞我？

漸漸的我發現
這些都不是我想要的
每日每夜更加困惑迷茫了

心裡就像有個無底洞
像是飄在海上的孤舟
像是飄浮在半空的氣球

也許我在等待另一個我
世界上的另一個和我一樣的靈魂
就像量子力學的另一半在同頻共
振

無論你在宇宙的任何一個地方
也許今生就會遇見你

真希望今生可以遇見你
不用再等幾世輪迴了

Through trials and tribulations, I've
tread,
Endured pain and hardship, life's path
I've led,
Circles and turns, days bustling with
strain,
Lost amidst it all, uncertainty's reign.

I've been on a quest, seeking life's true
meaning,
All I've witnessed and heard, feelings
intervening,
Yet the more I learn, the more I'm
perplexed,
Lost in the void, my heart feels vexed.

Always busy, the question persists,
What is it all for? I gently insist,
To amass more wealth, for treasures
untold?
Luxury brands, cars of silver and gold?

A larger, more lavish house to reside,
To be known and admired, globally
wide?
Gradually I've realized, it's not what I
seek,
Amid the daily whirlwind, I'm feeling
weak.

My heart feels like a chasm, endless and
deep,
A lonely boat adrift, the sea's secrets to
keep,
Floating like a balloon, suspended in the
sky,
In search of another soul, a resonance to
tie.

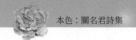
Perhaps I'm awaiting another version of
me,
A kindred spirit elsewhere in this grand
sea,
Like quantum entanglement, we'll align
and connect,
Across the universe, our souls intersect.

No matter where you are, distant or near,
In this lifetime, we might cross paths
here,
Oh, how I wish to meet you, this very
now,
No more waiting through lifetimes,
somehow.

75

露珠水境
Realm of Dewdrops

2023 年 6 月 13 日

無數個水境
隱藏在露珠之中
三千又三千
數之不盡

水境之中包羅大千世界
七色光下七色樓宇
亭臺樓閣美輪美奐
櫻花漫天搭出橋樑

消失在雲端直通天門
紫藤花漫山遍野
飄飄灑灑如雪如霧

鮮花水境各色精靈飛舞
香氣撲鼻沁人心脾
我們漫步在彩橋上

精靈在我們耳邊歌唱
排成各種形狀飛舞
花蜜流成清澈的河流
花型的小船隨風搖擺

花瓣的宮殿大氣輝煌
忙碌的精靈採摘仙果
鑽石般的明燈耀眼閃爍

七彩靈蝶煽動著翅膀
彈奏著迷人的琴音
粉紅色茶杯透著桂花幽香
如癡如醉　如夢如幻

異彩紛呈　變幻萬千
盡在露珠水境呈現

Countless watery realms, veiled in dew's
embrace,
Three thousand and three thousand,
countless to trace,
Within these waters, a universe
concealed,
Seven-hued lights, on structures revealed.

Pavilions and towers, beauty adorns,
Cherry blossoms bridge skies, a scene to
be born,
Vanishing into clouds, a passage to realms
high,
Wisteria cascades o'er mountains, a royal
dye.

Drifting like snowflakes, mist-kissed and
free,
In this watery realm, a tapestry to see,

Sprites in myriad hues, a dance in the air,
Their fragrant presence, beyond compare.

Upon bridges of color, we stroll hand in
hand,
Spirits sing by our ears, a symphony so
grand,
Shapes take flight, in wondrous array,
Honeyed rivers flow, in the sun's soft ray.

Petal-palace grand, in the heart of it all,
Sprites gather celestial fruits, at nature's
call,
Diamond-like lanterns, illuminate the
night,
A dazzling spectacle, pure and bright.

Rainbow butterflies, their wings aglow,
Playing melodies sweet, as they freely
flow,
Pink teacups whisper with osmanthus's
grace,
Enchanted by this dream, we find our
place.

A kaleidoscope of wonder, a myriad's
dance,
In the watery realm's trance, a mystic
expanse,
In dewdrop's embrace, a world to behold,
A symphony of colors, an enchanting
threshold.

76

全新的自己
A Brand New Self

2023 年 6 月 9 日

同過去說聲再見
如同鳳凰涅槃
浴火重生
破繭成蝶
遨遊天際
同所有的不開心說再見
明天是一個嶄新的自己

全新的心臟在跳動
蓬勃有力
全新的大腦在思考

嶄新的人生
全新的皮膚感受風的輕拂
溫溫暖暖
全新的味覺嘗遍世間美味
酸甜苦辣

你的每一天都是全新的
沐浴在晨曦的餘暉中
奔跑在海邊的微風裡
漫步在森林的嫩草間
徜徉在繁華的都市裡

我的每一天都是全新的
觀察著宇宙的浩瀚星辰
體會著聲音的波長形狀
好奇著酸鹼中和分子聚變
聚焦鏡頭記錄美麗瞬間

我們的每一天都是全新的
不再糾結過去
勇敢面對明天
用心去體會愛

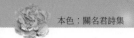

用善良的心去發現
這世界的所有美好
日月星辰的燦爛輝煌

In bidding the past farewell, we part
ways,
Like the phoenix's rebirth in fiery blaze,
Emerging from ashes, anew we rise,
Breaking free from cocoons, taking to the
skies.

Soaring through heavens, in boundless
flight,
Leaving behind sadness, a radiant light,
Tomorrow's promise, a brand-new start,
A canvas of potential, a masterpiece of
art.

A fresh heart beats, with vigor and
might,
A new mind's musings, an enlightened
sight,

A rebirth of being, a path unexplored,
Skin caressed by breezes, warm and
adored.

Taste buds awaken, flavors dance on the
tongue,
Sour, sweet, bitter, and the spices among,
Each day is a canvas, a creation unique,
Painted with moments, the vibrant and
chic.

Your days are all new, bathed in
morning's glow,
Running on shores where soft breezes
flow,
Strolling through forests, where tender
grass grows,
Wandering cityscapes, where life ebbs
and flows.

My days, too, are fresh, a cosmic array,
Observing stars in the night's grand
ballet,

Sensing sound's wavelengths, in
harmonious play,
Curious of fusion, where molecules sway.

Together we journey, through realms
unexplored,
No longer bound by what once was
stored,
Bravely facing tomorrows yet untold,
With hearts full of love, compassion to
hold.

Discovering beauty, with each kindness
we find,
In this world's embrace, its wonders
unwind,
The brilliance of stars, the moon's gentle
light,
Every day anew, our lives shining bright.

77

冷漠
Apathy's Embrace

2023 年 5 月 30 日

曾經炙烈眼光已不在
只剩些許的責任也不願承擔
明明說過一生一世相伴
短短幾年就天翻地覆

人與人之間更多是冷漠
更多的是人走茶涼　落井下石
僅有的一點純真無邪　也不在了
背叛誓言的代價　一點也沒有
看不出他的良心不安
僅有的愧疚也不在

189

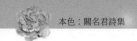

世事無常　變化萬千
也許永遠只是短暫的永遠
天長地久只是幾年的長久
剩下的只有　無情　絕情　痛的
發抖

曾經的朝夕相伴　被拋之腦後
不想提起　不再想起
撕心裂肺的痛　已經過去
獨自面對這個陌生的城市
獨自一個人面對生活的冷漠
要再堅強勇敢一些

不要怕

至少你擁有了自由
至少你還年輕
至少你還有夢想和希望
至少還有一個對的人在等著你
至少還有很多個明天和明天
至少還有健康　平安　寧靜的每
一天

不要放棄你的每一個美好的日出
和日落
看一看群山　璧水　鮮花　嫩草
的新芽
一切都會變的更加美好
是的
相信你自己

Once fiery gazes have faded away,
Leaving behind duties, you'd rather not
sway,
Promised forever, a lifetime entwined,
In just a few years, upheaval defined.

Humanity wanes into cold indifference,
Turning backs as tea cools, hearts lack
coherence,
Innocence lost, no longer untamed,
Betrayed vows and promises, unduly
unnamed.

Conscience untroubled, guilt fades from
view,
The fleeting bond shattered, feelings
askew,
Life's ever-changing, a constant array,
Eternal's a moment, a brief disarray.

Timeless devotion, a handful of years,
Only remains ruthlessness, torment that
sears,
Past's close companionship cast aside,
Unspoken, forgotten, those days denied.

Heart-wrenching pain, now echoes and
fades,
Alone in a city, estranged parades,
Facing life's chill in solitude's stride,
Summon your strength, let it be your
guide.

Fear not the path that lies ahead,
Freedom you've gained, a youth well-fed,
Dreams and hope still reside within,
Someone awaits you, a new chapter to
begin.

Countless tomorrows, yet to be found,
Health, safety, tranquility all around,
Cherish each sunrise, embrace each
sunset,
Mountains, flowers, growth's vivid
vignette.

Hold on to the belief in a brighter array,
In the end, all will surely convey,
Yes, believe in yourself, find your way,
For within you, strength forever will stay.

78

忍無可忍
Beyond Endurance

2021 年 4 月 10 日

忍無可忍
無需再忍

天知道什麼是對
天知道什麼是錯
也許沒有真的對
也許沒有真的錯

是的
十年磨一劍
你為了什麼

二十年的風裡雨裡
你為了什麼

勉強的笑顏
失去了顏色
每一滴淚都不會失色

表面也許就不是真相

忍無可忍
無需再忍

前路永遠是
正大光明

Beyond endurance,
No need to bear any more.

Heaven knows what is right,
Heaven knows what is wrong,

Perhaps there's no true right,
Perhaps there's no true wrong.

Yes,
A decade honing a blade,
What have you strived for?

Through two decades of storms,
What have you weathered for?

Forced smiles fade,
Losing their hue,
Each tear maintains its shade.

The surface may not unveil the truth.

Beyond endurance,
No need to bear any more.

Ahead lies a path,
Bright and true forevermore.

79

約定
Pledged Moments

2016 年 5 月

作詞｜關名君　作曲｜李東燊

我還在等待
你向我走來
沒有遺憾轉身
無話不說暢談
瀟灑自如不必顧忌太多牽絆
只因你我之間生命的約定
時刻記得你那黑色明眸在閃動
你的身影
誰懂我不斷向前
執著信念和約定

寂靜之間
你的誓言回蕩在耳邊
風吹向大海
雨朝我襲來
雷動響徹夜空
閃電照亮天際
訴說生命奇跡時間停在永恆
只因你我之間生命的約定
時刻記得你那黑色明眸在閃動你
的身影
誰懂我不斷向前
執著信念和約定
寂靜之間
你的誓言回蕩在耳邊
漂流茫茫人海中
不等滄海變桑田
終於站在你面前
說出久違的夙願
流星彙集雲端散發耀眼的光芒
只因你我之間前世的約定
無論身在何處飄流的心
已經找到了歸宿

只能見彩虹的另一端繫著我思念
黎明之前花瓣旋落在你的肩
只因你我之間生命的約定
時刻記得你那黑色明眸在閃動你
的身影
誰懂我不斷向前
執著信念和約定
誓言銘刻在心間
寂靜之間
你的誓言回蕩在耳邊

In the realm of anticipation, I remain,
Waiting for your approach, your name.
No regrets in turning, we converse
unbound,
Unburdened by constraints, laughter
resound.

With ease you stroll, unshackled and free,
Bound only by life's promise, you and me.
Always etched, your ebony gaze aglow,
Your presence, a steadfast river's flow.

Who comprehends my ceaseless stride,
With conviction and pact, side by side?
In quiet moments, your oath does sound,
Whispering through silence, all around.

Wind caresses the ocean, waves run deep,
Rain falls on me, secrets it does keep.
Thunder reverberates across night's
dome,
Lightning illuminates, guiding me home.

Voicing life's marvel, time stands still,
Bound by a covenant, beyond our will.
Your ebony gaze, an eternal sign,
In quiet moments, it intertwines.

Drifting amidst the sea of countless faces,
Unyielding to change, firm in my paces.
Finally standing before you, the end is
near,
Long-lost wishes escape, sincere.

Stars converge above, a radiant display,
Past lives' covenant, lighting the way.

No matter where my wandering heart
roves,
Found my haven, where love behoves.

Only the rainbow's end my eyes can see,
Tethered to thoughts, across eternity.
Before dawn breaks, petals descend anew,
Carrying memories, our love's residue.

Life's pledge engrained within my soul,
As quiet prevails, your words console.
In the tranquil between heartbeats' beat,
Your promises echo, melodies sweet.

《本色》
——關名君詩集（中英典藏版）

Eternal Hues: The Poetry Collection of Lotus Guan (Bilingual Edition)

作者： 關名君 Lotus Guan

作者商業合作郵箱： searong777@163.com

編輯： 青森文化編輯組

設計： GERY RABBIT STUDIO 卷里工作室

出版： 紅出版（青森文化）

地址：香港灣仔道 133 號卓凌中心 11 樓

出版計劃查詢電話：(852) 2540 7517

電郵：editor@red-publish.com

網址：http://www.red-publish.com

香港總經銷： 聯合新零售（香港）有限公司

台灣總經銷： 貿騰發賣股份有限公司

新北市中和區立德街 136 號 6 樓

(886) 2-8227-5988

http://www.namode.com

出版日期： 2024 年 7 月

圖書分類： 文學／詩集

ISBN： 978-988-8868-10-0

定價： 港幣 128 元正／新台幣 510 元正

Eternal Hues:

The Poetry Collection of Lotus Guan

(Bilingual Edition)

Eternal Hues:

The Poetry Collection of Lotus Guan

(Bilingual Edition)